The Case of the Purloined Parrish

By

Alma Gilbert

Published by Alma Gilbert Books & Publishing

Rancho Palos Verdes, California

Distributed by Create Space, a Division of Amazon

ISBN: 10:0692319530
ISBN-13: 978-0692319536

DISCLAIMER

THIS IS a work of fiction based on some of the author's life experiences of forty years in the art and museum world, using purely fictional characters in imaginary locations in New Hampshire and Vermont. Other than the Cornish Colony American artists mentioned here, including Maxfield Parrish, Augustus Saint-Gaudens, etc., and their works, and Vermont mystery writer Archer Mayor, any similarity to any other persons living or dead is purely coincidental.

THE AUTHOR wishes to thank Vermont mystery writer Archer Mayor who in a moment of madness permitted her to use his name and to make him a character in this work of fiction set in the art world of New England.

ALMA GILBERT

THE CASE OF THE PURLOINED PARRISH

BY

ALMA GILBERT

DEDICATION

This book could not have been completed without the help of My Dearly Beloved Husband, a born techie who understands and speaks to computers (although I've heard him cussing them sometimes). When megrims, gollywobbles and other pesky computer glitches cause me to lose chapters at a time and disappear into the nether regions where lost chapters go to cavort, he would find them and make them re-appear with his investigative ministrations to my machine, supposedly one of Apple's finest.

My husband Peter is the stand in for my character of Bert Lincoln. He, too, served on our museum's board of directors. To him and to all that he represents in my world, I dedicate this, my first fiction book.

The Author

LIST OF CHARACTERS IN ORDER OF APPEARANCE

Mary Margaret Winters (Maggie): Elderly Director of a small Vermont museum

Denny Grant: Faithful museum grounds keeper and jack-of-all-trades

Dorothea Granville (Dotty): Maggie's oldest friend and donor of an important painting

Connie: Youngest and most promising of the museum's cadre of volunteers

Samantha Vanderpool: Newly elected President of the museum's Board of Directors

Bert Lincoln: Retired Navy captain, member of Board of Directors and Maggie's best friend

Jeff Andrews: Museum staff photographer and restorer

Amy Brown: Maggie's secretary and museum bookkeeper

Hughie Roberts: Past museum Board President and current Vice-president

Katherine Clark: Museum Board member and Treasurer

Constance Brown: Museum Board Secretary and mother of Amy Brown

Prudence Cartwright: Owner of art galleries in Chicago and New York

Lester Wonkrowski: Chief assistant to Prudence Cartwright

Mike Walters: Vermont police officer

Vito Lipinski: An expert in breaking and entering and other less palatable jobs

Mr. Jones: Anonymous and moneyed client from Chicago; prospective art purchaser

James Duncan: Retired Dartmouth art history professor and newly elected Board member

Ronnie Santini: Vermont restaurateur and newly elected Board member

Detective Lieutenant Lucas (Luke) Lucarelli: from the Montpelier barracks

Rick Dupreville: Museum counselor and former N. H. State Attorney General

Special Agent Dyer: FBI fingerprint expert

CHAPTER ONE

Before she had really awakened this early morning, Maggie Winters was aware of the musical chatter of myriads of birds willing the sun to awaken and peer into the remaining patches of winter snow interspersed between mud and emerging green grass surrounding her cottage. She loved hearing the chatter and peeps of baby birds urging their parents to go foraging for them and bring home, if not the bacon, at least a tasty bird morsel to share with their brood. Her bed was warm and the cozy comforter she had worked on with the Ladies Quilting Society at the museum extended the invitation to linger a little longer before testing the coldness of the floor next to her bedroom slippers.

After saying some leisurely morning prayers, she extended a foot experimentally out of the covers to "test the waters" so to speak as her maternal grandfather, a crusty Portuguese whaler would have said. The temperature this cold Vermont April morning met all her expectations of frigidness. Spring was just around the corner, but no one had informed Mother Nature of the date on the calendar. Resolutely, she tossed the quilt covers aside and slipping on her bunny house shoes that her grandchildren had given her to "keep Granny's toes warm," she shuffled towards her dressing room for her robe and start her daily ration of coffee ready for her breakfast. Maggie was definitely aware that nearly pushing the grand old age of 70 sure made a body a lot creakier than in years past, particularly this early in the season. One thing that helped her get a move on every day was the particular pleasure she felt in still being able to work at the museum where she had been its curator for nearly the last forty years…or at least close to 40 years since she had taken the position after the untimely death of her husband, a respected physician in a Boston traffic accident.

She had been hired by the small rural museum in Vermont which specialized, like its brethren, the larger museums in the New England area, in the works of the artists of the Cornish Colony, a particular specialty of her American art history knowledge. The remoteness of the area where her museum was sited made its exhibit season shorter to conform to Mother Nature's whims and long Vermont winters. Her season began in early May, but the packing, shipping of art works and the preparation of catalogs and exhibit spaces consumed her days in March and April until the roads were a little more passable both for tourists and for other visitors. Once the plows left the roads in peace, one could expect the flocks of visitors who traveled yearly from as far away as California, Oregon and Washington to see the beautiful art works of such luminaries of the American Cornish Colony area like: Augustus Saint-Gaudens, James Earle Fraser, Thomas and Maria Dewing, George de Forest Brush, but most specially, her favorite: Maxfield Parrish.

Maggie had seen the young and old lovers of Parrish art come into her museum and stand gazing before one of his beautiful compositions with those famous blues that F. Scott Fitzgerald had immortalized in one of his novels with the words: "...as blue as a Parrish sky..."

She had actually lost count of how many times she saw a viewer dab his or her eyes after contemplating a particular work that brought a memory of light over a beloved landscape viewed as the artist depicted. That made her job even more worthwhile despite the old fashioned and rather small salary she still was able to pull from the Board of Directors each year. Of course, one of the other perks was that the Director's Cottage, situated within the Town limits near the museum, had been and still was a part of the compensation arrangement. But best of all, she got to enjoy the paintings and sculptures of her favorite artists as they rotated year after year in the museum exhibits which she organized.

Today was going to be a special and exciting one. She had been tracking a shipment of art that Federal Express was to deliver that morning. It contained a small but marvelous little Parrish oil, one of her favorites called *Dingleton Farm* that was being loaned by the widow of a former museum trustee in Rhode Island for the upcoming Spring Exhibit now just around the corner in May. The work was one of Parrish's favorite ones. It had been done when the artist was 86 years old, and he had kept it in his studio's living room until the time of his death. Maggie had a photograph in her office of Parrish standing next to *Dingleton* while speaking to visitors in his

3

studio. The little oil done in the spectacular Ultramarine Blues that Parrish favored, showed a local farmhouse nestled in the hills of New Hampshire where the artist lived, along with the rosy rays of a breaking sun illuminating the barn, house and surrounding snow with the warm light and the promise of a new day.

Her coffee was ready and its heady aroma permeated the little cottage enticingly. She finished her toilette and gave her short hair a lick and a promise with the brush. She inspected the results critically and deemed them tolerable. Her face was still relatively wrinkle free thanks to good genes and a fidelity to Oil of Olay since her 20's. She smiled as she noticed that most of her iron grey hair still had a crown of silvery white curls that framed her face: "Grandma's Halo" as her grand children had dubbed them. "Humph!" she snorted to herself, not much of a halo when faced with recalcitrant board members who liked to wave museum bills in front of her nose as if she was personally responsible for incurring them.

Come to think of it, maybe she was, after all she was responsible for putting on the yearly exhibits to attract visitors, the life-blood of any museum without a healthy endowment to keep it going. Maggie fought like a tigress for her museum and many a time she knew she was getting in several of the board members' gun sights, figuratively speaking, of course!

After a quick piece of buttered toast with sugar and cinnamon to make it special, and her rationed two cups of decaffeinated coffee, and her myriad vitamins to keep the "ol' bod" moving, she brushed her teeth and grabbed the keys to her Subaru (an absolute necessity if one lived and worked in rural New England). The museum was sited in the former home of one of the artists of the Cornish Colony with a spectacular view of the Connecticut River Valley dividing New Hampshire and Vermont and the grand old Mountain of Ascutney, overseeing the magnificent landscape below.

She made it to the foot of the hill in four minutes flat, a record time she thought happily, and began the iffy ascent, dodging mud holes made by the melting snow. "I made it!" she grinned happily at the thought of again conquering the rough ascent and relaxed her death grip on the steering wheel. Not a happy thing to get stuck in the mud while going up the hill. It had happened to many others, including her several times in the years she had been there. She liked to remember the old Walt Disney movie where a little train ascends a precarious hill thinking to itself: "Can I make it up? Can I make it up? Can I make it up? I THINK I can! I THINK I can! I THINK I can!" Maggie pulled up to her Director's parking spot and sighed contentedly. She thought "If I can conquer that blasted hill, the rest of the day will be a cinch, recalcitrant board members or not!"

Signs of activity met her at the entrance. Denny, the faithful "Keeper of the Grounds", was already there with his crew cleaning up the debris that winter had left of branches scattered around, a displaced stone on the walks here and there, and myriads of wet leaves uncovered after the snows had begun to melt. "Morning,

Denny!" she called cheerily. "Morning, Maggie! Nice day today. You expecting a delivery or visitors so I can spread some sand on the hill?"

"I think so, Denny. Just Fed Ex with a delivery and hopefully some volunteers to help me start unpacking and seeing what's going to go where." she replied. Denny nodded knowingly and began preparations to sand the driveway.

The museum housed a permanent collection of several pieces of Cornish Colony art, both pictorial and sculptural. Each year, depending on the theme to be presented, Maggie scoured other museum's collections and made endless calls to private owners, cajoling loans of priceless works from them. Everyone said she had a unique talent for getting people to part with beloved art objects on a yearly basis so that they could be displayed and enjoyed by others. The love of the art, particularly the myriad collectors of Maxfield Parrish art, were for the most part, willing to lend their works so that others could enjoy them as the owners did. They knew that Maggie was a protective presence and most of them trusted her implicitly with their loans. Of course, their loans had to be insured for their full value, and many times that was problematic, since major works of artists like Saint-Gaudens, Dewing, Fraser, Remington and Parrish were now appearing at the auction houses and in the powerful art galleries of New York, Dallas, Chicago and San Francisco with astronomical six figure prices.

The question of fully insuring the pieces that were being loaned was always a sticking point in the craw of

6

recalcitrant board members. Many times, it was necessary to use a portion of the insurance that protected owned art objects of the museum in order to cover adequately the insurance of pieces that were being loaned by the owners of the art. Principal private lenders of art to the museum included the names of titans of commerce, industry, banking and commerce. The most generous to date had been the heirs of the Gertrude Vanderbilt Whitney family, with their treasure trove of Parrish murals and paintings.

The little painting Maggie was expecting today was from a private collection of a good friend, now from Carmel, California with whom Maggie had gone to school eons ago. Dorothea Granville (Dotty to her friends) was also getting of an age, like Maggie, and enjoyed knowing that some of the artworks she and her now deceased husband had bought early on in their marriage were appreciating in value.

Maggie walked into her office and dumped her purse under her desk where no one could see it and where it would be accessible to her if she needed something.

She quickly scanned her desktop phone answering unit (no iPhone for her, thank you!) for messages and seeing nothing startlingly urgent proceeded to sit down and review her upcoming schedule for the day. After finding out that there were no outstanding messages she needed to return, she proceeded with the pleasurable task of reviewing what she had on hand for the upcoming exhibit and what must be unpacked and sorted out today.

She had donned sensible shoes and work slacks for the day's labors. When the call came that Federal Express had arrived and needed her signature, she rushed breathlessly to meet the driver and her awaited package.

"Morning, Maggie! Expecting something important? It requires your signature." The Fed Ex drivers all knew her well enough to go on a first name basis. After a little back and forth banter on the state of the hill, the economy and the upcoming exhibit, the driver collected her signature and handed her the expected package. Large museums had a shipping and collecting department. Most rural museums did not, but the "Next Day" delivery drivers for all the major companies like Fed Ex, UPS or even the local post office knew the routine and sought the person in charge for delivery of rush packages which usually came in special art conveyance "Strong Box" boxes that included specially designed foam padding under the regular cardboard to protect their precious cargos.

The box was small enough so that Maggie could carry it to the room where the packing crates, boxes and containers were stored. When the box was expertly and carefully opened by the resident restorer, Jeff Andrews, Maggie could barely contain herself and lifted the small, approximately 11" x 15" oil on board, from its cradle in a bed of specially cut foam to cushion its ride. "Look at it!" she crowed triumphantly! "Isn't it gorgeous? Let's look at it in natural light to see its true colors!"

Of course, it is a definite "No-No" in the art world to expose major paintings to sunlight, but a quick look to see the absolutely gorgeous tonality with which Parrish imbued his paintings was accepted. "After all", Maggie reasoned to herself, "the artist had made an actual skylight in his studio so that he could paint and examine the works he was creating under natural light". It never failed. When a new work arrived at the museum, particularly a Parrish oil, an adoring group immediately sprang out to examine it and OH and AH in delight.

"There's a letter in the box addressed to you, Maggie", Connie, one of her young assistants noted, picking up the envelope that had been enclosed under the painting.

"Probably the signed loan agreement and the insurance evaluation", responded the director. "Let me take a quick look to make sure all the information is in order."

Maggie took the envelope from within the packing and walked towards the window in order to have better light. She put the letter down after reading its contents and turned to face her three assistants with a look that they could not at first interpret. "Anything wrong, Maggie?" As was her custom, Connie took the lead and queried their director. Maggie's lower lip was trembling, and then broke out into one of the sunniest smiles the volunteers had seen in a long while.

"Nothing is wrong, dear! I just can't believe our good fortune! My friend Dotty from California is making the museum a gift of this painting. She says it deserves to be viewed and enjoyed by a whole bunch of people instead of just her. She adds that in her heart, she always saw it coming to us one day on a more permanent level instead of just the occasional exhibit loan. I just CAN'T believe it! Oh, Dotty! How kind and also how just like you to do this without any prior announcement or commitment."

Maggie's lower lip trembled and she hurriedly wiped an unaccustomed tear that threatened to spill unbidden down her cheek. "I must call and thank her, right away! Oh, wait! No. It's only six a.m. in the West Coast. Dotty is certainly not up yet. Better notify the board first and call the museum's insurance to add it to our in house art inventory." Still clutching the little painting against her breast, Maggie hurried back to the office to call the president of the board.

Normally, calling Samantha Vanderpool, the newly elected president of the museum board was not one of Maggie's favorite things to do at the start of the workday. Mrs. Vanderpool, a recent retiree newly arrived from the New York financial circles, had not yet mastered the enviable task of realizing that life in New Hampshire and Vermont was not to be lived at the frantic breakneck speed which New Yorkers were accustomed to. Things were more leisurely here, and well, one required a certain amount of tact and politeness not really needed in the Big City. At almost five feet eleven, she towered over the miniscule and elderly museum director who, could at best, in her most elevated heels, maybe reach a height of five feet one.

"Yes, Margaret, what is it?" was the brusque opening when the phone was picked up.

"Sorry to disturb your early morning coffee, Samantha,"

was the answering reply from Maggie." But I have wonderful news! The museum has just received the gift from one of our proposed lenders to the exhibit. It's the Parrish oil *Dingleton Farm!* She's making a gift to us of this gorgeous work that she and her husband acquired from the Parrish estate in the early 70's!" There was a brief pause as if Mrs. Vanderpool was checking her memory to see if she even recalled what this painting looked like, and not finding it in her newly acquired memory data base of Parrish works that she had actually seen or been made aware about, her answer was cool and almost disinterested.

"That's very nice, Margaret, but the museum board must at first pass judgment on the intrinsic and monetary value of the gift before it can be accepted. Remember, please, that we cannot carry a large inventory of owned art because it would make our insurance premiums very precarious."

Maggie could not believe what she was hearing. What person outside of one residing in an asylum for the mentally unbalanced would not be thrilled and delirious to know that a Parrish painting probably worth in the low six figures had just been gifted to them? For a couple of ticks, Maggie was speechless, which did not occur often in the span of her lifetime. "Samantha, the board need not pass on the intrinsic value of this work. I do. Trust me, it passes hands down. All you and the board have to do is smile, and write an immediate letter profusely thanking the donor for her generosity to us. Then, you can find in the most expeditious manner any funds necessary so that we can add the new painting to our insurance policy."

There was a brief pause in the conversation and then Samantha responded in her most icy tones: "I will make sure to pass your recommendation to the board as soon as we meet tomorrow. In the meantime, my dear Mrs. Winters, kindly refrain from telling me my job and for making any plans for hanging *Dingleton Farm* until it has been duly approved for acceptance by a majority of the board members." The phone clicked off and the connection was broken.

A polite knock at her office door preceded a head with shimmering silver hair who greeted her with a grin and twinkling, happy eyes set in the frame of a man who had either put in long hours on a tennis court or sailed a great deal. In fact, he had done both. "Heard the good news about *Dingleton* when I stepped in the door of the museum, but Hey! You look as if you just took a bite out of a slice of lemon! What gives? You should have your dancing shoes on and be doing a fandango on your desk!" The silver hair gent that walked in the door was Bertram Lincoln, (Bert) one of Maggie's best friends and stalwart companion, another 70 something who volunteered not only time on the board of directors, but also was on dock when the time came to take down or put up exhibits.

Bert was a Massachusetts native son, direct descendent of one of George Washington's generals. He had served in the Navy and still loved sailing his beloved gaff rigged Cat Boat during summer weekends when he was not volunteering as a docent in the museum. His summer home in New Hampshire and a penchant for history had translated into working as a volunteer at the museum and later being asked to serve as part of the Museum Board of Directors.

"Just spoke to Samantha to impart the good news and it was lucky that I left the conversation with my head still on my shoulders! She snapped at me and seemed not at all happy about our new gift", said Maggie, whose aggrieved tone of voice left no doubt that she had definitely not expected such a cold reception to what was literally one of the best gifts the museum had received in a long time.

"Don't fret, Maggie! She's still feeling her way around and probably doesn't realize the value of the gift received. She hasn't pored through many of our library books and is just coasting on what an inheritance and a generous alimony can do. She has not yet suffered any of the slings and arrows that it takes to run a non-profit in New England and is used to the tough New York type of brusque mannerisms we don't much cotton to around here." Maggie made a face at him but his presence and obvious enjoyment of the news did much to lighten her mood.

"Thanks, Bert! I needed that. You're right. She's still pretty new and hasn't learned to handle associates in a polite Boston type of mannerly way. I'll get over it! You will soon probably have a call or a text from her informing you of the news and calling for a board meeting to approve or reject the gift."

"Reject the gift? Are you nuts or something? Why should we reject the gift?"

"Maybe because we have to find extra money to add it to our Museum's Owned Art policy," was the tart reply.

"Hell, Maggie, we can find the money. All she has to do is hit the tried and true donors including Yours Truly to get it done. It's just a premium adjustment, we're not looking to buy the painting, its OURS!"

"Bert, you have a way of stating the obvious that is very endearing, and I thank you for it! You have lighted my mood immensely. Hey, how about if this lady buys you lunch at our local diner at noon today. Will that prompt you to volunteer to help hang some paintings and move some sculptures around after I feed you?"

"Ah, Maggie! You know how to touch the right chords of a hungry man's heart to make him do your bidding. You're good at that, you know?" Maggie smiled, and gave him a playful swat. "Go on, with you! I've got work to do before lunch. See you noonish at our usual table?" His smile and a wink answered her as he walked out of her office. With a much lighter heart, Maggie began to review for the fifth or sixth time her list of what art was going to be installed where.

CHAPTER TWO

After a satisfying lunch of sandwiches and coleslaw followed by a chocolate bar for energy which she and Bert shared, they stopped by her office to pick up *Dingleton Farm* and take it downstairs to have it photographed by Jeff Andrews, museum photographer and installer. The little museum, like many other rural New Hampshire and Vermont non-profits, was open only May through October so they kept a very small staff of workers on their payroll. Besides Maggie as Director, only Denny, the grounds keeper, Jeff Andrews, the photographer/installer and Amy Brown, their secretary and bookkeeper made up the year round staff. The rest were a cadre of volunteers who helped with mailings, installations, phone answering, gift shop attendants and tour guides during their season.

Jeff had already been alerted that *Dingleton Farm* was "in house" and needed to be photographed, both for the upcoming catalog and to provide to the museum's insurance carrier. He truly was a whiz with a camera. The Parrish paintings were by far the most challenging to photograph because of the myriad of layers of varnish that the artist built into his creations. Jeff was one of the few photographers who had had the pleasure of photographing literally hundreds of Parrish works that were either owned outright in permanent collection or had been loaned to the museum during its lifetime. When Bert and Maggie walked in with the painting, he was waiting for them with an easel, camera and lights at the ready.

"I'll bring it back to you in the main exhibit room after I finish photographing it. Are you going to hang it right away or do you want to store it in the big vault for a while?"

The museum owned a massive vault that measured almost 9ft by 10ft. It had been brought in originally by the first owners of the house in the mid 1860's and was too large to be taken out when the house changed ownership in the early portion of the 20th century, so it had become the winter storage for the museum's collection of owned art works as well as incoming works for the next exhibit. When the paintings were stored there as opposed to being on display, their insurance premiums reflected a certain amount of reduction. There were no shipping crates stored in the vault. Only paintings in their individual boxed containers or small sculptures were wintered there. The larger sculpture pieces, like the eight and a half feet by five feet bronze Augustus Saint-Gaudens *Diana of the Tower* remained on the museum floor since they were too massive to move.

"Let's try seeing where it's going to be sited during the upcoming exhibit, Jeff", was Maggie's response. "We'll save the space for when we get an O.K. to accept it after tomorrow's board meeting."

"Hey, Maggie! Don't fret, we'll approve it, that's for sure", was Jeff's quick reply. "I've done my due process of calling a few of the board members before lunch to prepare them for the good news. Remember, there's nine board members and we only need a quorum of five 'Yeas'. I talked to three members who are very excited already. I make the fourth vote. I know we can get one more on our side. What's not to like about the deal?"

Maggie, as Director of the museum, could only advise and suggest courses of action. Being a paid employee, she had no vote (although she told herself, she certainly had a voice and the board members were going to hear her loud and clear). Sometimes attending the board meeting was agony for her: seeing some of her pet projects sometimes going the way of the flesh, since there was a finite amount of money to fund them. She thought of which board members were going to be likely to vote against accepting the painting after hearing Samantha's argument that they could simply not keep on adding expensive art works to their owned works that were being insured. There had to be cap room left under their insurance to provide for "wall to wall" coverage for the objects which they were borrowing from lenders each year. She mentally reviewed how the board might vote:

President Samantha Vanderpool was against it. One Nay. Hughie Roberts was Vice-president this term. He was last term's President, but as the one who had recruited Samantha hoping to have her bring some of her inherited and/or divorce settlement cash into the

17

museum's fund raisers, he was probably going to go with her and vote Nay. Then there was Katherine Clark, French Canadian Treasurer of the board. She, of all people would strongly veto any further expense: Another Nay vote.

The Board's Secretary, Constance Brown was the mother of the museum's Amy Brown, the museum's secretary and bookkeeper. She would probably be a Yea. It was going to be a close vote with one swing voter. Maggie felt her tummy constrict and told herself there was no use worrying about it until it happened.

She busied herself checking off the items from her lists that she wanted on the three main exhibit rooms and supervising the packages that were being brought in either from storage or from the vault to be unpacked near where they were going to be installed. Denny, Bert, Jeff and three volunteers were all busy seeing to it that all the items on her list were now present and accounted for on the museum floors. Denny and Bert, the "muscle" of her little band of helpers paired together to bring in some of the heavier pieces. Jeff helped with smaller works and the volunteers set up the table for the opening of the storage boxes by Maggie. It seemed like a little well-oiled machine that had been doing this for several years. One of the younger volunteers had brought in a radio that was set to play some of the music the young people enjoyed. As long as it was not a booming thudding beat, Maggie accepted it with resignation, knowing that kept the younger helpers happy and returning to help year after year.

By close to five o'clock when the evening lights had already been turned on outside of the museum, Maggie and her little band of helpers had just about completed the installation following the design she and Jeff had worked out in detail before starting.

Maggie wanted the art up so that the board members would see it the next day before their board meeting and perhaps slightly influence their vote. After all, she reasoned that it would be difficult to resist a Parrish original hanging on their wall with the full light of museum installation highlighting its beauty? Anyway, they had requested that the work be loaned for this exhibit, so it was there, occupying its rightful allotted space. Whether they had to return it after the end of the exhibit or keep it as part of the collection pretty much depended on how the vote was going to swing the next day.

After thanking the volunteers and her staff for their hard work, Maggie saw everyone out with the exception of Jeff who needed to tinker a little bit more in his dark room with the transparencies he had taken of *Dingleton*. Maggie knew it was usual for him to stay behind and then lock up again after he left. He and Maggie were the only ones with keys to the main door where the alarm key pad was installed and which had to be set every night by the last person leaving. Maggie collected her purse and some papers she wanted to take home to review and called out to Jeff: "Getting ready to leave, Jeff. I'll lock up but not turn the alarm until you go. Don't forget to turn on the alarm!"

"I never forget, Maggie. Don't worry! Good night and prepare for your meeting with the board tomorrow!" With his parting words still resounding through the now darkened hallway, Maggie checked the door one last time to make sure the locking mechanism was on, and went out slamming the door to make sure that the locking mechanism was in place before turning towards her car and walking briskly holding her warm scarf around her face to prevent the cold April night winds from turning her nose the color of her reddish woolen scarf. "Good night, Museum. Be well", she whispered as she turned the lights on in her Subaru, and started the slow descent down the hill.

CHAPTER THREE

  Maggie had been able to negotiate the redoubtable hill that
led to and from the museum with a modicum of grace.
Denny's sanding had done the trick and allowed her winter
tires to get a better grip on the mud and mud holes.   She had
just pulled into what passed as a driveway to her little cottage,
when she heard her landline ringing inside.   "Who'd be
calling me at supper time", she wondered ticking off in her
mind the possible people who might be calling. Dropping her
purse on the entry rug, she kicked the door closed and
grabbed the ringing phone.

  "Where were you?" the warmly familiar voice of her friend
Dotty from California demanded. "It's WAAAY past your
bedtime there and I've rung you three times."

  Maggie smiled inwardly. Of course Dotty would begin a
conversation with a question! "Just got home from the
museum. Stayed late to begin the installation of the galleries
and Dotty, THANK YOU!!! for the unexpected and totally
generous gift to the museum!   I was going to call you
tomorrow after the board meets to approve your gift and
thank you profusely and promise you chocolates, wine, and a

lobster dinner next time you come."

"I could settle with an introduction to one of those good-looking strong and silent men that populate the area where you hang your hat these past few years."

"Don't know many of those except Bert Lincoln, and I wouldn't want to share him with you of all people."

"You never were much fun, even in school! I was never able to introduce you to the Lend-Lease concept of sharing good looking guys....but, hey! I didn't stay up to call you at ten pm your time just to discuss the men of our lives." Widowed some years back and now at a grand 72 years, Dottie still talked a good line.

"Yeah, I thought this might be a tad late for you to be calling. I KNOW you always track the paintings you send and know that they have been received safely, so it's not that. What's got your dander up at this hour?"

The tone of Dotty's voice became instantly serious. "Listen, Maggie. This is important. Sit down and get comfy because I know you must have just pulled in and we need to talk about something private but very important."

"I'm sitting down Dotty. Just kicked off my shoes and put my feet up on the recliner. What's on your mind?"

"O.K. Maggie. Let me talk this through with you. It's about *Dingleton Farm.* You know that I was eventually meaning to get that donated to the museum so that others could enjoy it as much as have. Well, the gift idea got the green light a few days ago way ahead of schedule. There's this pushy woman art dealer from Chicago who's been pestering me to sell the painting to her for some time. I've always declined her advances and offers and put her off saying I had still not made up my mind what to do with it. The last time I said that, I must have pushed her buttons or she has someone who's seen it and told her he wants it and is offering a heck of a lot of money, in order for her to keep coming after me"

"That's not unusual in the art world, Dotty. If a dealer knows she can double or perhaps even triple the value of a work, they CAN be a tad aggressive in trying to get it."

"I told you to listen to me. Let me finish, O.K?"

"Sure. Sorry."

"This art dealer I was telling you about must have hired a couple of low life thugs to watch my house. I had seen their decrepit car parked down the road for the past few days and I live in a cul de sac in this very tony section of the Carmel Highlands where usually only the people who live here park. Most of us drive Mercedes or BMW's up here and that car looks as if it's ready to be junked". (Well, that's no crime", thought Maggie wondering what her friend was going with the conversation).

Dotty continued "About three nights ago when I was happily ensconced watching my favorite CNN program, Champ, my very protective Boxer, started emitting this low growl in his throat. At first it started to creep me out, and I told him to quit it several times, until all of a sudden he sprang up and pushing the screen door open was out like a flash growling and barking to wake up the band! I don't know about the band,

23

but all of a sudden I see all my neighbor's lights go up on their porches wondering what Champ's fuss is all about. I was watching TV in my bedroom on the second story, so when I pushed the curtains aside to see what was going on below, I came face to face with those two low life characters that Champ had just treed in the pine that's by my bedroom. I grabbed my cell phone and called 911 and those guys must have been on patrol nearby, because within a minute or two their car pulled up in my driveway and they were using their flashlights to see who Champ had treed up that tree"

"Oh, Dotty! How scary for you. What did the police do?"

"They knocked on the kitchen door and asked for me to let Champ back into the house so they could get these guys down. I guess neighbors had complained about the car that had been parked there for two or three days with these rascals inside, so they had been watching."

Maggie interrupted the narrative again because she was upset for her friend: "Did they take the guys in for Peeping Toms"?

"No. It gets better. It seems one of them had a rap sheet a mile long and they had been eying where I had *Dingleton Farm* hung. It seems someone had offered them a tidy little sum to "pick it up" for them and they thought that after I went to bed, they could come in via the terrace from the tree and jimmy the French doors open, grab the little painting and scuttle out. They weren't very smart and were not counting on Champ having other ideas on their plan. But that motivated me that since I had targeted the work for your museum anyway, this was as good a time as any to send it to you on a more permanent basis."

24

Maggie felt she was sounding like a broken record by saying "Oh, Dotty! How awful for you to go through that. Are you all right?"

"Yeah, it made my adrenaline kick in, all right. So I decided there and then, I'd toss the football to you and let you handle it from now on." She giggled at the use of the football term. Maggie knew her predilection for her beloved SF 49ers! Taking a breath, Dotty continued, "Now listen, Maggie. I called the gallery of the pushy art dealer and left a message that I had made up my mind and had decided to donate the work to your museum. That I had sent it out and she and her prospective client could go enjoy it when you open your upcoming exhibit."

Maggie was still upset that her friend had received such a fright and was concerned about her welfare. "Are you SURE you want to do this, Dotty? You could lend it to us long term, you know."

"Yeah, I know that Maggie and I can tell you I considered it. But we're not getting any younger and this has been targeted for you and your museum, so there you have it. I have plenty of other art hanging on my walls. I will miss it, I grant you that, but maybe when you have the time, you could make me a good print copy from the original and I could hang it back here again in its old place in the den."

Maggie agreed readily and after a few more minutes on the phone with her friend while they were saying their good-byes, Dotty seemed to remember one more thing: "Listen, Maggie, do you still have the cell phone your kids gave you?"

"I do, Dotty, somewhere. I don't like the gadgets!"

"Do me a favor: Take it out, make a habit of charging it every night and keep it in a pocket on your jeans, pants, sweater, whatever! But keep it on your person. You never know when you might need it and not have a land line handy. Promise you'll do that!"

"Oh, O.K. if it makes you feel better, I'll try to remember to do just that but what a nuisance!"

"Don't care! DO it!" Dotty used her command voice, so Maggie knew it was important to her.

"I'll do it for you, dear. Now, I've kept you up. Go to bed and a million thanks again. You'll get a letter with slavish thanks for the board, but you know I OWE you one! Good Night, Girl!" With that, the two friends hung up the phones and Maggie went to brew herself some Chamomile tea and mull over her friend's words.

CHAPTER FOUR

  The next morning, after going through her purses to see where she had left the cell phone the kids had sent her one Christmas, along with the charging contraption that came with it, she dropped it in her big carry all purse. Maggie had packed her lunch, and after tidying up her kitchen she headed out towards the museum a little earlier than was her practice. The day looked as if it would be quite eventful, with the board meeting, the "show and tell" as she liked to call it of the new exhibit areas that they had prepared the day before, and the other myriad tasks associated with hosting a board meeting that afternoon.

  When she stepped out to her car, she noticed that despite what the calendar on her wall said, that it WAS the month of April, there had been a slight frost, so she needed to scrape her windows and turn on the defroster inside her car. Grumpily, she went ahead and started the tedious scrapping of her windshield, calculating that the precious time she had hoped to have of a few minutes quiet in her office to digest the evening telephone with her friend must instead be used in scraping the windows of the Subaru. After a few minutes of more mulling and grumping to herself, she was off to face the hill once more.

Good old Denny, she thought once she reached the obnoxious up hill climb. He had gotten up even earlier and sanded it down for her, knowing full well that it would be highly slippery with frost. She parked her car in the museum's little space, and noted that Jeff had evidently already arrived since his car was there. She fumbled with her door key, mentally preparing herself to find the alarm already turned off since Jeff had beaten her in the door.

Maggie was startled to see the pulsating red warning light indicating the alarm was still on and she hurriedly keyed in the code to keep the obnoxiously loud alert from sounding. She absolutely ABHORRED the noise it made.

"Jeff!.. Jeff." she called out several times and met only silence. Where was he? Since the alarm was on, he could not have come in. Yet his car was in the parking space. Then she heard the rattling of a key chain out doors, and the stomping of boots wiping out the ice before entering and then the door swung open and Jeff stood there looking puzzled.

"Hi, Maggie! Just getting in?"

"Yeah, saw your car and thought you were already in, but the alarm was on, so I was wondering where you were."

"Just looking around the periphery. Saw a lot of skid marks coming up the hill probably before Denny had sanded and I looked around to see if there were anyone here. There's tire tracks on the ice around the museum, so someone's been around having a look-see way before we open. It's not even 7:30 yet. Not a local person surely. Everyone knows the museum is not yet open and the volunteers don't get here until nine. Wonder who it was? Evidently, they did not find anything open, saw the light from outside that the alarm was on, and went on their way."

"Gee, that IS odd. Let's ask Denny if he saw anyone around when he was sanding," Maggie managed to say, but her mind was preoccupied with the past evening call from Dotty. "No. This is Vermont, not New York or California. We don't have people trespassing and mucking around this early in the morning." she told herself. "Dotty's call must have me on edge. Better not let my fancy get out of hand or I won't get anything else done today!"

With this, she picked up the purse she had dropped on the ground when she was keying her code into the alarm panel and marched resolutely to her office upstairs. As she passed the exhibit spaces, she could not help herself taking a mental inventory on what they had hung the evening before making sure everything was in place. Everything was just as they had left it the night before. After dropping off her lunch in the refrigerator in the staff room, she headed straight for her office and immediately immersed herself with answering call backs, listing her priorities for the day, checking on the catering for the board meeting that afternoon and reviewing what was on the agenda for the board later that day. It should be an interesting afternoon.

Her secretary, Amy Brown arrived promptly at nine and asked if she wanted either some tea or decaffeinated coffee that she had just perked. "Did you get the last message I left on your desk last night, Maggie? It was on a post-it note. Mrs. Vanderpool wanted you to call her immediately when you walked in today. I told her you were downstairs setting up the exhibits and she told me that today would be fine."

Maggie looked around, found the post-it and called the president of the board. "Morning, Samantha. You wanted to speak to me?"

"Yes, Margaret." the cool voice seem to make an attempt at warming. "Didn't want to disturb you while you were hanging the exhibit, but I wanted you to know that we need to add two guest chairs at our boardroom table. We're having two distinguished visitors from New York come in after our board meets and I needed to make sure that you had enough refreshments for all of us."

"Thanks, Samantha. I'll notify the caterers right now to add a few more sandwiches and some more hors d'oeuvres, so we should be fine. Anyone we know coming?"

The president of the board seemed somewhat taken aback by her query. "I don't know if you've met the lady and her assistant. She's a very important art dealer from Chicago that called me recently and asked if she could be given the courtesy of being allowed to present a proposal to the board."

Something lurched in the pit of Maggie's stomach when she recalled her evening's conversation with Dotty. "Hmm," she managed to say. "In the course of my 40+ years in the field, I've met a lot of important art dealers as well as museum curators. I wonder if that's Prudy Cartwright? I used to know her when I worked as a consultant in Boston in one of the galleries on Newbury Street." She said this with a lump in her chest. It HAD to be the dealer Dotty had called her about.

"I didn't know you knew Mrs. PRUDENCE Cartwright."
Samantha answered with a pronounced accent on the more
formal "Prudence". She is now very respected and established
owner of major New York and Chicago galleries.

"I knew her before she owned the gallery and was not yet
married to the then owner, Mr. Cartwright, whom I believe
was quite elderly or ill at the time of their wedding", Maggie
answered. She thought: it must be one and the same....it
WAS a small world.

"Well, I'm glad you two know each other. See you shortly
before five when I start the meeting." With this, Samantha
hung up the phone abruptly leaving Maggie jittery and with a
nagging feeling of unease. Her well developed "Mom-has-
eyes-in-the-back-of-her-head" sense of perception was sending
very definite "Danger! Danger!" signals to her hopes of having
Dingleton Farm at the museum on a permanent basis. What
would Dotty say if these people got their hands on it, after all?

CHAPTER FIVE

The day passed without any more distractions. The caterers arrived with the added request to the museum's order, which was promptly refrigerated in the Staff's Break Room.

Maggie had tried in vain to get hold of Bert Lincoln without success. He must be out of range with his cell phone, or left the pesky contraption behind when he went fishing prior to coming home and changing for the board meeting. She did not dare broach the subject with any of the other board members. It would seem too much of "insider information" that she did not feel good about releasing until Samantha opened the subject of "New Business" and introduced the letter of Deed of Gift that Dotty had sent to the museum along with *Dingleton Farm* itself.

A little after 3:30 that afternoon, Jeff poked his head in her office and asked if anyone had talked to Denny about the tire marks and footprints around the periphery of the museum early that morning.

"I put in a call to Denny about that, but since he'll have to work late closing up the gate at the foot of the hill today because of the board meeting, I think he may have gone home early this afternoon for his supper and did not get my message," responded Maggie.

"Well, good luck at the meeting. Break a leg or something, Maggie, but see what you can do to twist some arms about coping with the extra rise in the insurance if we accept *Dingleton* for the permanent collection. I just adjusted the lights in the room where *Dingleton* is hung and it looks terrific! That baby just seems to glow with an inner light of its own!"

"It may very well have a little extra light of its own, Jeff. Some of the Parrish oils seem to have an extra aura about them given all those additional coats of varnish that the artist put in them between different layers of paint. The colors then remained pure from the tube and did not 'muddy' each other. Did you know that upon occasion and on special paintings to him he would grind miniscule particles of the precious jewel lapis lazuli to mix with his blues? It's a secret he kept for his favorite works and that famous 'Parrish Blue' tonality that Scott Fitzgerald coined in one of his books describing a spectacularly toned sky."

"Didn't know that, Maggie! No wonder his paintings are so hard to photograph and seem to throw light back at you. You've cleared up the mystery for this particular photographer, thanks! Anyway, going home a little early since we all worked late last night. As I said: Break a leg!" and with a wink at the director, Jeff closed her office door and left whistling down the hallway.

At exactly five o'clock, Maggie, a devout church goer, offered up a quick prayer for help from the Holy Spirit, asking for inspiration to know what to say and how to present the idea to the directors. She made the sign of the cross over her forehead, gathered her purse and her folio for the presentation and marched out to greet the first arrivals.

 Predictably, Bert Lincoln was one of the first to arrive followed in close succession by some of the board officers and other members. Samantha always liked to make a grand entrance and would show up when she calculated that all the board was in and were waiting for her entrance to begin the meeting. Maggie fussed around making sure all had copies of the agenda that Samantha had sent earlier via e-mail to be copied by the secretary and have ready at each board member's place along with a pitcher of cold water and glasses at each chair. Seeing that all was in order, she sat in her usual place next to Samantha's position at the board table. She, as a paid employee did not have a vote, but as Director and responsible for the smooth running of the museum and its small cadre of personnel, she needed to acquaint board members on the upcoming exhibit and report any other pieces of news relevant to the running of the museum.

 Samantha Vanderpool arrived a few minutes later and with a great show of shuffling papers in front of her place at the table she called the meeting of the board of directors to order. The minutes were read and the treasurer gave the members the latest numbers in the museum's shrinking bank account. Katherine Clark was a retired CPA and a very capable and no-nonsense treasurer. She was more involved in the bottom line than in the vagaries of the esoteric and emotional facets of running a non-profit museum whose mission was to preserve the art in its keeping, enhance its collection with loans of art relevant to it's mission from institutions and private lenders and still keep its bank account out of the proverbial soup. She was perfect for the job.

All proceeded according to Robert's Rules until it came time for New Business to be introduced. The letter from Dorothea Granville offering to donate the Parrish oil *Dingleton Farm* to the permanent collection of the museum was read and the buzz and excitement it created was palpable. Maggie allowed her thumping heart to hope for an acceptance of the gift from the board, when, upon the President's asking for discussion before the question of accepting the work was put to a vote, the Treasurer raised her hand to speak.

"Maggie, do we know what the approximate value of this proposed gift is?"

Maggie swallowed hard and announced that she had looked through the various sales of art at the different auction houses and the value of a Parrish landscape painting that had not been reproduced and had been created in the latter years of the artist's life would be in the mid range between $400,000 to $600,000 for that small size. When that number was met with a gasp from the board, she wondered if she should tell them that Christie's in New York had just sold a 23"x 18" Parrish landscape oil titled *Peaceful Valley* done in 1952 for over a million dollars. That would really scare them off!

"We'd never be able to cover the insurance premium for that kind of value in addition to our own collection of what we're already covering," was the Treasurer's immediate response. "We have more room to put it among the pieces we're covering just for a few months for this upcoming exhibit, if it's in the collection of a lender and not in that of our own

35

institution".

Maggie knew that was coming, but was still a shock to hear the gift possibly being turned down because the museum could not afford to own it and pay the insurance for it.

Unexpectedly and seeming to come from nowhere in particular, Samantha Vanderpool spoke and said: "It would be an affront to the donor to have it turned down. We should try to explore other avenues to raise funds so that we can make room in our own museum collection value for this valuable little jewel."

Maggie was blown away by this sudden change of heart from the President. She looked around and saw heads assenting in unison. Hughie Roberts, the board's past president was bobbing his head like a car's Bobble Doll gone wild. "I totally agree with Madam President's thinking. We can always do a fund raiser to pay the silly insurance price hike in order to have such a crown jewel in our collection!"

"Would any one of you like to make a motion to that effect? " "I so move!" crowed Hughie. "Second it" was Bert Lincoln's quick motion.

"All in favor, raise your hand." Eight hands went up including the President's. "Opposed?" Katherine Clark primly raised her hand.

"Motion to accept this kind gift is passed" intoned Samantha in her best presidential tones. Constance Brown, our secretary will record that we have moved to accept this generous gift and will be instructed to write the donor thanking her for her magnificent gift to this non-profit immediately."

Maggie was so astounded, she could only smile at Burt and shake her head in disbelief. They had made it and *Dingleton Farm* was going to belong to the museum in perpetuity.

"Unless, there is any other pressing new business, we will take a ten minute recess and return to meet some distinguished visitors from New York that are honoring us with their presence." announced Samantha.

"Oh, NO!!!" thought Maggie, suddenly cold with apprehension. "Samantha couldn't, she wouldn't do that to us…." Her eyes locked with Bert's who looked puzzled at the sudden change in his friend's demeanor. He motioned her to go out momentarily for some fresh air and inquired quietly what the heck was going on with her. That's what they had been hoping to have happen and now that it had, Maggie looked as if her best friend had died.

"What just happened here, Maggie? I thought that's what we were hoping to have happen. What's bothering you? If it's finding the extra money for the insurance, I'm sure some of the board members can kick in with some donations, and since our esteemed President of the board is hot to have it happen, she can also jolly well contribute to the kitty for the insurance."

"It's not that, Bert. I had a long talk last night with the donor and she told me a Chicago based art dealer had been pressurizing her to sell the painting to them and she didn't like their underhanded tactics, so she chose to donate it to us now, as opposed to a few years from now. I think these are the

37

same people she was talking about."

"Well, then…why did Samantha put the matter on speed dial and had it pass so quickly? Wonder if the 'distinguished visitors' have discussed with her why all of a sudden they chose to drive up from New York to meet with us yokels in Vermont? I don't like the feel of this, Maggie."

"You may be right, Bert, but let's not worry until we see what they have to say. Let's get back to the board room and meet these good travelers from the halls of commerce and see what they have up their kister."

CHAPTER SIX

Maggie and Bert made it back to their seats and waited until Samantha walked in to the board room accompanied by a man and a very well dressed woman wearing, of all things, high heels which were a little the worse after negotiating the mud and muck from the car to the entrance of the museum. The visitors were found the extra seats that had been brought in for them at the right hand of the presider. All eyes were on the two visitors and looked up expectantly for Samantha to introduce them. Occasionally, prospective board members or possible future donors were introduced to the board and of course were always met with interest and attention. Samantha gaveled the table unnecessarily since all eyes were on her and introduced the newcomers.

"Esteemed members of the board, it is my distinct pleasure to introduce to you our visitors, Prudence Cartwright, a distinguished and respected gallery owner with locations in New York and Chicago and this is her able assistant who drove her here, Lester Wonkrowski."

The couple were received with polite applause and the

:

board settled in to hear what their president was going to say about them.

"I heard from Mrs. Cartwright just two days ago when she called and said she was interested in our little non-profit's work and would like to be of assistance in seeing that if possible, she'd attempt to help us maintain our mission of bringing important art of the members of the Cornish Colony to our visitors here in Vermont in this beautiful small museum. Mrs. Cartwright is bringing a very interesting proposal for our consideration, so without further comment let me ask her to address you."

Prudence Cartwright rose from her seat and smiled to all those present. Her eyes stopped briefly on Maggie and her head nodded a slight greeting to her. "Thank you, Madam President. I have the pleasure of congratulating your able Director, Margaret Winters, and all of the members of your board for her recent acquisition of that wondrous little oil by Maxfield Parrish titled *Dingleton Farm*. It is quite a coup for a small non-profit institution to acquire such an exquisite little work. Mrs. Winters and I knew each other a long time ago while we both worked in Boston, didn't we Maggie?" Maggie nodded imperceptibly to acknowledge that.

"We went our separate ways, she to this wonderful little museum in the hills of Vermont and I to the world of commerce in New York, and subsequently Chicago, where as you probably know, I head a pair of prestigious art galleries patronized by the wheelers and dealers of the world. I am also considered to be the ultimate Purveyor to the Stars in Hollywood when it comes to their acquisition of fine works of art."

 She stopped briefly to take a breath and shift a little of
her hefty weight from one slender mud covered shoe to
another. She patted her very expensive and exquisitely
coifed wig and proceeded with her prepared remarks. "I
would also like to introduce my able assistant, Lester
Wonkrowski, who is known as my "Expediter". He makes
sure that everything progresses for me the way it should,
don't you Lester?" Lester acknowledged the introduction
with barely a nod, not bothering to smile or make eye
contact with anyone in the room. His tall, spare form
gave the impression of strength combined with a little
brutality. His dark knitted eyebrows seemed permanently
furrowed in a frown and he seemed to only be interested
in mentally evaluating who was in the room and where
the exits were located.

 "My interest in the continuation of your mission is one of
the reasons we're here, isn't it, Lester?" Lester managed a
nod without looking at anyone directly. Prudence pressed
on, "I know how tough it must be for little non-profits to
continue to maintain their work in these tough economic
times" She looked around for confirmation, but to their
credit, the board members still wanted to hear her out
before they agreed to her perceived summation of the
state of their finances.

 "I have come to offer a small proposal for your able
consideration. I am prepared to write a donation check to
the museum to cover all the expenses for the insurance of
your new acquisition during the upcoming exhibit." She
paused for effect and to elicit polite applauses to her

proposed donation. She received it. It was a welcome gift, but not unusual for what the museum received donation-wise. Smiling broadly, which made her face break into several wrinkles, she pressed on. "That's not all I'm prepared to do, however." A stirring of interest caused the listeners to shift in their chairs slightly. "I am prepared to offer this non-profit a cashier's check for half a million dollars, payable at the end of the exhibit you're currently preparing, for the little Maxfield Parrish painting *Dingleton Farm* whose gift from its past owner, I understand you have just accepted."

There was a stunned silence following her proposal broken only when a smiling President of the board rose to speak. "Mrs. Cartwright, that's a very tempting and generous offer that I'm sure the board will take into consideration and we're grateful that you would consider helping a small non-profit like us with your generosity. Of course we will give it its due consideration and respond to you once the board has had a chance to deliberate. In the meantime, we will be happy to accept your initial donation to cover the value of the insurance on *Dingleton Farm* during the exhibition scheduled to start in a couple of weeks. We will be back to you with the board's decision within three or four days via registered mail to your address in Chicago or New York, whichever you prefer. In the meantime, please join us with the delicacies that have been prepared for the board members."

Polite applause ended the deliberations since the board seemed still to be in shock at the proposal of having half a million dollars in their shrinking bank accounts by the end of the exhibit when the painting which just had been accepted into their collection could be turned over to its new owner. The first board member to gather her wits was Katherine Clark, the board's treasurer, who quickly collected the proffered donation to cover the insurance for the painting during the exhibit from Prudence Cartwright before she and her "Expediter" left the room.

When Katherine returned from seeing the two guests off, the board was still in a state of shock from the events of that evening: first the donation of the painting by its former owner, and then an immediate offer from a gallery owner to buy the same painting for half a million dollars, was a bit too much for their normal agenda.

"I can't believe what just transpired. In the history of this little museum's board, I don't think we have seen this much action since the last Hurricane!" was Bert Lincoln's slightly sardonic comment. "I've learned in my young and unpretentious life when something looks too good to be true, it generally isn't!"

Samantha Vanderpool looked like the cat which had eaten the canary and enjoyed it very much! Her grin from ear to ear left no question that she was pleased with the proceedings. If one were to look around the board table, the only mournful face was Maggie's. "Madame President", she addressed Samantha, "may I address the board with a recommendation?"

"Of course, Maggie. You have the floor and our rapt attention."

Instead of addressing the board from her seat at the table, Maggie rose to speak. "You are aware, of course, that as members of the American Alliance of Museums we are bound by the rules and regulations established by the AAM regulating the treatment of donations of either money or art objects. There are some stringent rules on de-accession of donated items. If the item donated to a non-profit is part and parcel of the mission of the non-profit, it cannot easily be deaccessed. Only with objects that are not materially related to the mission of the museum and only in times of great financial need can an object be released from the museum collection and then only at an open major auction, where the public is informed of what is being sold and by what institution and the amount it fetches. It cannot be sold to individuals, much as the museum would want to do so."

Total silence was met after the announcement. Constance Brown the museum's secretary and bookkeeper and mother of Maggie's personal secretary, was the first to speak. "Well, easy come, easy go, but at least we own a very delightful painting and have a check to insure it, to boot! All's well that ends well, I say!"

Katherine Clark, the ever practical board Treasurer, spoke, voicing probably what was going on in several of the members' minds. "I'll deposit Mrs. Cartwright's check at our bank tomorrow first thing before she changes her mind once she finds out she might not be getting "our" painting." The meaning of the possessive pronoun she used was not lost on Maggie, who smiled at her and then smiled at Bert. Maggie was taking the first free breaths

since the announcement that an offer on the painting was
made by Prudence Cartwright.

 In looking around the board table, she was struck by the
glowering looks that both the President and Vice
Presidents were throwing her way.

 "Mrs. Winters, (Maggie noted that the president had used
her formal name) are you sure about your facts? Can you
provide a copy of the particular AAM regulations for the
board to see?"

 "I can, Madame President. If you allow me two minutes
to run to my office and fetch the official AAM manual, I
will be pleased to quote chapter and verse both to you and
the board." With this, Maggie turned quickly, almost
upsetting her chair and marched upstairs faster than she
though herself capable of doing. Switching on the lights
in her office she went straight to her bookcase and
withdrew the AAM manual, a heavy tome of probably
300 or more pages, and almost took the steps back down
in record time for a near 70 year old.

 She laid the official manual in the middle of the table and
quickly turned to the section on deaccessions. It was there
in black and white. She offered the book pointing to the
pertinent chapter for the Secretary to read to the board,
and sank back down to her seat, breathing the first real
sigh of relief since Prudence Cartwright and her
"Expediter" whatever his name was, had entered the
room. After the Chapter and Verse on deaccessions was
read, there were several moments of total silence in the
room. The first to speak was Katherine Clark, a crusty

French Canadian if there was ever one.

"Darn it! I was already seeing myself running to the bank with that big old $500,000 check to deposit it in the museum account, but I guess we won't be doing that now," she sighed disappointedly.

"Madam President", Bert addressed the crest fallen Samantha, "In light of the museum's charter regulations, I now move that we write Prudence Cartwright thanking her for the generous offer, but declining to accept it in view of the regulations and guidelines that museums belonging to the AAM must follow regarding the selling of previously donated objects in our collection."

"So Second." Katherine Clark said sighing audibly.

"Discussion" ordered the President.

"Don't see how we could do anything else but decline the sale, given the rules and regulations binding us governing such actions, " was the dispirited contribution from the Vice-President, usually Samantha Vanderpool's strongest ally. She called for a vote which to Maggie's great relief was unanimous.

"So ordered", was spoken in quiet resignation by the presider. "If there is no further business to discuss, the meeting is adjourned." Not much was being said as the board members exited the room, everyone was exhausted and still trying to make sense of what had just happened in the boardroom.

Bert gave Maggie a quick hug and asked if she had her
46

wheels or needed a ride down the hill. "My car is there, Bert, thanks for everything tonight."

"That's me all over, Maggie! Rescuing damsels being threatened by fire breathing dragon ladies from New York. Call if you need anything in the museum tomorrow. I'm free all day."

"Thanks, Bert. I'll call before nine in the morning if I need your presence at the museum."

He waited until all the lights were turned off in the exhibit spaces and she had set the alarm before pulling away in his car.

CHAPTER SEVEN

The next day dawned with all the splendor of a promised spring in the not too distant future. The birds all seemed to be coming back in and congregating in a rush to get things going: finding mates, building nests, nagging the morning with their voices to come and light the way for them. Spring was definitely beginning to assert itself in the weather. On her way to work, Maggie had noted that flocks of wild geese were flying back, skimming the shore of the great Connecticut River calling to each other. Driving by River Road on her way to the museum, she saw that the ponds were beginning to thaw so the croaking of frogs could be heard even through the closed windows of her car. Spring was her favorite season, despite the mud and the rains that thawed the remnants of snow patches into the ground. Spring meant renewal, new beginnings, and having a beautiful Parrish oil to greet her arrival at the museum made her euphoria with the season even greater.

After a running start, Maggie negotiated the seemingly vertical ascent of the hill with a minimum of fishtailing from her trusty Subaru. O.K., maybe that was one of the small things she didn't like about spring: the ubiquitous mud that could be a drag to anyone's spirit.

Maggie was at her desk still feeling a definite lift in her spirits the enjoyment of an early morning spring day in New England always brought to her. She plugged the coffee machine, dropped her massive purse under her desk and remembered to plug the cell thing contraption the kids had given her that passed for a telephone. One of the first things that caught her attention was the whirring of her FAX machine in the next room. It was from Constance, the board secretary asking her for the specific quotation that prevented the board from accepting the offered tendered by Mrs. Cartwright the evening before.

Maggie brought out the ponderous AAM regulations and quoted the three relevant issues in the section on deaccessions that applied to the museum and the art object in question:

> *1. Deaccessions should not occur when the work in question is relevant to the institution's mission.*
> *2. Deaccessions should never be prompted by changes in tastes or expressions of interest from individual collectors or dealers.*
> *3. Deaccessions must conform to the wishes of the donor(s) of the works from which they were acquired.*

She copied the applicable rules and included a copy of the donor's letter where Mrs. Granville was expressly requesting that her gift be retained by the museum as part of their permanent collection of important Cornish Colony artists such as Maxfield Parrish. She added a note

49

of her own, that thus far, because their values had risen prohibitively, the only ones in their collection were two early works that had been donated by former owners of the mansion that housed the museum.

Since the check that Prudence Cartwright had given to the museum the night before was generous, Maggie reminded herself that she must update the value of the two other Parrish originals in the museum collection so that they could also have a new insurance value as part of the collection. She dashed off a quick e-mail to a friend working in the American Art Department at Christie's Auction House in New York, and asked if he would consider rendering an opinion on the value of the two other Parrish originals which he would know well from his visits to the museum and its laudable collection of Cornish Colony artists.

After doing that she scrolled down to read her messages and answer the usual inquiries that would come in from the museum's website asking for directions, hours of operation, Opening Day events for the upcoming next season, etc. Among the messages there was a brief e-mail from her Jeff asking her to call him at home since this was his normal day off.

She glanced at the clock at her desk and judging that Jeff would probably be up and around by then, she dialed his number and waited for him to pick up.

"Hi, Maggie! You're at work early again. How did the meeting go? Any problems with our 'friends' from New York and Chicago?"

"Nothing that cannot be worked out, Jeff. I'll tell you when you're back here tomorrow. Did you have something else in mind"

"Maggie, I need to run this by you. *Dingleton* should be cleaned up and made spiffy before we open in a few weeks. So as not to spoil the exhibit that we have already set up by taking it down, why don't we have a giclee made of it from the very good photo I took of it yesterday? We could put it in the original's frame so the press or anyone that needs to take pictures of the exhibit prior to our opening can have an image of *Dingleton* present and accounted for."

"I think that's an excellent idea, Jeff. It hasn't been cleaned since 1958, so it is definitely needed. Thank you for suggesting it. However, it is too valuable an artwork to be left lying around in your studio at the museum while you're cleaning, varnishing it and letting it dry. If you place it in the safe each night before you leave work, I would let you clean it now. What do you estimate it will take to do a thorough preparation and drying time?"

"No more than two weeks at most, Maggie. We have time if you let me get started ordering a giclee from that guy in Claremont, NH who's done some work for us framing and doing giclees when the museum needs them. He's usually got a lot of work because he's good, but he tries to squeeze time out for the museum if we need it in a hurry. We can certainly keep the original in the safe every night."

The mammoth safe had been originally installed in what

used to be the library. It had been there since the 1860's. The original owner had served in President Lincoln's cabinet during the American Civil War. He kept many of his papers and documents there for safekeeping, and presumably also bulky art works of value when the family was in residence in Washington instead of Vermont. Only three people in the museum knew the combination to the massive safe: Maggie Winters, as Director, Jeff Andrews as the Restorer, Photographer and Installation expert and whoever was currently President of the Board for the term. When a new president was installed, the museum's combination was changed, so only three people remained permanently responsible for its valuable contents.

It was agreed to proceed with Jeff's suggestion of ordering a giclee and installing that in the frame of the original painting while it was out being restored of any minor nicks or painting loss as well as cleaned and varnished, so that it's full beauty could be enjoyed by the visitors to the museum.

Maggie worked diligently until lunch time on the press releases announcing the opening of the upcoming exhibit as well as showcasing the donation of *Dingleton Farm*.

She took a look at her window and longed to eat her home-made chicken salad sandwich outside. The lovely springtime feel, the white birches getting feathery around the edges and even the mud beginning to dry up gave her hopes to see the first blush of emerald green grass sprouting on the brown hills. That promise of spring led her thoughts to Bert Lincoln's company. She had enjoyed their meal together earlier in the week and wondered if he might be interested in having his lunchtime repast with her outside on the patio benches that Denny was just beginning to bring out after their winter sojourn in the museum's barn.

In the precise instant of her thoughts of inviting Bert to join her, her phone rang. It was her friend from Christie's with a recommendation on the values she had requested earlier on her e-mail to her. After the usual conversation of acquaintances that had not spoken for a few months, her friend suggested a value for the two other Parrish originals in the museum's collection.

"Maggie, as you probably know, those two paintings owned by the museum were works on oil done on stretched paper in 1904 for the Eugene Fields book: Poems of Childhood. As such, their worth today would be in the mid six figures range. They could possibly fetch more once people got started bidding. I would hope if the museum ever wishes to deaccess the paintings, you would consider Christie's to do it for you."

"Thank you! That's higher than what I thought, but since they're an integral part of the mission of this museum, I doubt that they would ever go for sale unless we hoped to acquire another more valuable piece of art from any one of the artists of the Cornish Colony. However, if that ever happens, you know I would recommend Christie's auction house. I am grateful for the information, though!" After a few more polite inquiries about their families and the state of the weather in New England, her Christie's friend who was a native from the region rang off.

After a few more moments of introspection, Maggie decided to look up the amount for which the two other Parrish paintings were currently insured. Just as she was firing up the current insurance values carried by the museum for their important art works in the collection, her phone rang and her secretary Amy Brown announced that she had a call on her private line from a member of the board.

With a little feeling of misgiving, Maggie picked up the phone to find out that the caller was Bert Lincoln asking her if she felt like talking over the previous night board fireworks over a sandwich out of doors. In her relief that it was not bad news coming in that might in any way impact or prevent their acquisition of *Dingleton*, Maggie accepted with alacrity and promised to meet him downstairs in the museum garden benches within fifteen minutes. Since Bert lived just five miles away across the Connecticut river in New Hampshire, she knew that fifteen minutes would be ample, particularly the way he drove his small sports car.

Sure enough, when she went downstairs, Bert was already there and had commandeered one of the best tables that Denny had placed underneath the large oak shading the museum garden. He, too, had brought his lunch as well as some fresh peaches he had picked up in the market probably sent from California so that New Englanders would see what they were missing by not living in the land of warm sunshine and little mud.

"Looks like as if everything went swimmingly last night," was Bert's cheery greeting.

"I hope so, Bert. Truly I do, but I have a nagging feeling that Prudence Cartwright will not take this lying down. She and her "Expediter" friend are very persistent and won't go quietly with that rejection of their offer." Maggie then proceeded to fill Bert in with the full details of the conversation that she had had with Mrs. Granville, the donor of the painting, a few nights back and the low life hoodlums that her dog had chased up a tree outside her home. "I have the very awful feeling in the pit of my stomach that they were going to try to steal the painting for those awful dealers."

"Maggie, they couldn't sell the painting once the newspapers trumpeted it had been stolen!"

"Bert, there are collectors out there who pay a so-called "professional thief" to steal an important painting for them, and then display it in a secure place in their home where they don't invite others to view it. This is opposed to the understandable pride of someone actually buying them and then wanting to share their acquired treasure with their family, friends and acquaintances. Look at the Parrish murals that the artist created for Gertrude Vanderbilt Whitney! The two massive works that you remember we had the honor to display for one season at our museum here, were loaned by the new owner to a gallery in Los Angeles where they were on display. They were stolen from there in 2001 in a theft worthy of the Thomas Crown Affair movie. They're still missing and the FBI lists them in the flier they send out to museums every once in a while, as two of the ten top Art Thefts still at large."

"Yeah, I guess I had forgotten about that art crime theft. I read they disabled the gallery's alarm over a weekend when they would be closed, created a hole in their ceiling and then rappelled two stories down to the galleries where the murals were being displayed. It seems such a shame what they did to get them out! I read in the papers that they had actually CUT them out of their large frames, rolled them up and again rappelled back out carrying the rolled paintings with them. How big were they, do you remember, Maggie?"

"Of course, I remember, Bert! I also remember what a devil of a time we had when they were loaned to our museum and we were doing the installation. The murals measured five and a half feet tall by eight and a half feet wide. They were brought to the museum rolled up by the conservators. The massive standing frames were almost ten and a half feet high and had to be brought in dismantled and then assembled by their craftsmen once they had been brought into the museum's show room."

Maggie shuddered thinking that the theft could have happened here, in this remote little museum in Vermont. As she remembered seeing the glorious Vanderbilt murals displayed in the main exhibit room, a shudder of premonition hit her, making her reach for the sweater that she had discarded when she sat outside in the garden.

"I'm cold all of a sudden, Bert. Let's go indoors and get some coffee in the staff room."

"Maggie! Don't worry! This is not New York or Los Angeles. This is Vermont. This type of crime does not happen here!"

"I sure hope you're right, Bert", answered Maggie not being sure at all.

Before he left after getting some coffee, Bert, sensing her moment of fleeing panic, gave her a comforting hug and asked her to call or e-mail him if more "he-man" volunteer work was needed. She smiled gratefully at him and told him that for the time being, she and the lady volunteers who were helping with the mailing had everything in hand and filled him in about Jeff's idea of making a giclee of *Dingleton* and hanging it "in situ" while he cleaned, did minor restoration and varnished the painting in preparation for the opening.

"That makes perfect sense, Maggie. In case reporters come before the actual opening to review the show, they will see a full exhibit and since the giclee is the closest thing to an original that exists, they won't be able to tell the difference unless they want to examine it with a magnifying glass. Then when the exhibit opens to the public, the original *Dingleton* will emerge from its trip to the "painting beauty spa" all spiffy and glorious."

Seeing him pull out in his sporty little Triumph, Maggie gave a quick prayer of thanks for having such a wonderful friend who was also a dandy eye treat, if she allowed her mind to wonder in meadows it had no business viewing. Must be springtime priming up my forgotten juices, she counseled herself judiciously.

Sighing deeply, she turned on her heels and ascended the

stairs back to her office and her ever expanding to-do list of things to be completed before the opening of a new season and a new exhibit, with a scrumptious Parrish painting in their collection.

Bert, in the meantime, went home wishing he was a poet with a pen holding a quart of ink to sing the praises and odes to the season and present them to Maggie to lift her mood. Unfortunately, the roof of his beautiful and historic home across the river in Cornish was leaking like a sieve and needed immediate attention. His ode to spring and Maggie's gentle beauty and strength would have to wait until his more worldly and pressing needs of his house and roof would abate. The ravages caused by a winter in New England must be remedied immediately. Whistling, he crossed the 100 year old bridge between New Hampshire and Vermont and turned his mind to more constructive paths.

CHAPTER EIGHT

Prudence Cartwright stretched lazily in her modern living room penthouse apartment atop one of New York's tonier sky rises with a view of Central Park. She shared her living space with Les Wonkrowski as long as he suited her fancy. Because of her wealth acquired over years of maximizing the prices of expensive paintings in her New York and Chicago galleries, the young woman from Peoria, Illinois who had interned along with Mary Margaret Winters at the Boston Museum of Art many years ago, had morphed into a sixty something woman with demanding tastes in both art and men. Prudence scratched her lank over colored thinning black hair. The expensive wig she liked to wear made her scalp, damaged after years of coloring, constantly itchy.

"You've got a call from the gallery in Chicago", announced Les bringing her cell phone to her and adding: "Put your damn wig on! You look a mess!"

Prudence cast him a venomous look, but did not put her wig on. "We're not on Skype, dummy! They can't see me on the cell phone!" She snatched the phone from his

hand and began the conversation with a peremptory:
"Yes. What is it?"

 She nodded two or three times and then spoke curtly.
"Tell him I'll call him back as soon as I hear. I'm trying
to get the damn painting from the museum and made
them an offer, but tell him it's going to be pricey." She
ended abruptly and handed the cell phone back to Les.
"Call the New York gallery and see if they have any mail
or messages from that museum."

 Wordlessly, Les touched the speed dial and was
connected immediately. After speaking briefly, he
returned, "They have a letter for you that was delivered
via Fed Ex from Vermont. Must be from them. Do you
want them to open it and read it back to you?"

 "Yeah. Have my secretary call me back on my secure
landline." Les complied and then tossed the cell phone
back to her. "Get your own calls! I'm not your
secretary." With that, he left the room. Prudence could
hear him slamming the front entrance as he left the
apartment without further comment to her. Within
minutes the NewYork gallery called her back. "You
want the whole thing read back or just the short and
sweet summary?" the assistant manager asked. "Just tell
me: are they willing to sell it or not?"

 "Doesn't look like it. They quote AAM regulations
preventing them from selling that particular piece of
donated art, so if you want it bad enough you may have
to go with Plan B that you cooked up when they jailed
those two dummies in California you insisted Les hire to

case the house of that old broad who had it in Carmel."
The man who spoke was another one of Lester's hires
from Newark, NJ, and although made an assistant
manager, he had not yet learned the refined techniques
that it took to schmooze prospective clients with what he
called "high falutin'" dialog and sales pitch. That task
belonged to her cadre of cultured young women from
some of the better art colleges that Prudence liked to hire
to add touches of refinement to the faces and voices of
her employees who dealt with the buying public.

Prudence slammed her cell phone down after cutting off
the dialog of the "assistant manager" that Les had hired.
He was reputedly from one of the gangs operating out of
Jersey who had made the transition to the more civilized
centers of New York, but who brought the work ethic of
"my way or the highway" with him to his new job.

The woman who had been brought up by a family of
strong (some said bull-headed behind their backs) no
nonsense mid-western folks that for two generations had
worked in the manufacturing plants of Deere Tractors,
did not take "NO" as a viable answer. She stabbed the
cell phone with her long, perfectly manicured hands and
speed dialed Lester.

"Wazzup, now?" was the curt answer. "Plan B, Lester"
was all that Prudence said.

Then she added "I'll catch a quick flight up to Vermont
tomorrow and set the stage for that myself before these
idiots can screw it up again. But first let me do some
schmoozing with the prospective buyer over the

phone."

  Prudence's clients included a plethora of unlikely
individuals, from wives of tough Chicago mobsters to the
more effete clientele of Hollywood, or as she liked to have
her people call her: " Art Purveyor to the Stars". These
were people who had earned vast sums doing relatively
little themselves but who had the good fortune to land
juicy roles that made them vast amounts of money. The
client she had to consult had made himself a certain
reputation in Chicago that made him conversant with
high paid lawyers as well as to some of the less reputable
of his brethren in that tough and divergent city. His wife
was more interested in the art that could be found in
highly expensive jewelry stores. He had found a niche
for his money in art that conveyed beauty and serenity
not usually found during his workday. The landscapes of
Parrish with their depictions of homes and nature in
quiet surroundings, gave this particular client a sense of
inner peace and escape that he could not have with the
type of job description he gave to himself.

  He was not one used to being denied, so Prudence was
favored with some less than respectful language and a
vague threat of dropping her from his favored suppliers.
This served to motivate her even more to again drop in
at the Vermont museum and get the lay of the land, so to
speak, so that Les's job might go a little more smoothly
than the last time. She had her secretary at the New
York gallery get her tickets to the Lebanon airport, which
although it was located in New Hampshire, was only
about fifteen minutes away from where the museum was

sited across the river in Vermont.

  She also made provisions to have a car waiting for her at the airport so that she would not be at the mercy of the occasional taxi that ferried people back and forth from the airport to their local destinations.

CHAPTER NINE

Maggie was awake very early the next morning. Partially responsible for that was the knowledge that the museum had scheduled a walk through by members of the press prior to opening to the public within a couple of weeks. She was grateful for the free publicity that the regularly scheduled Thursday Art sections in the local papers would provide for the exhibition, such as **The Valley News** from Lebanon, NH and the **Rutland Herald** from Vermont.

The birds outside her window had been at it since before five and their enthusiasm for the coming of the day was palpable. Everywhere, you could see the buds beginning to swell and the green spreading over the brown hills surrounding her house and the museum.

While thinking what she would say to the reporters who were to call on her later, she recalled with amusement a quotation from one of Maxfield Parrish's letters in the museum's archives written late in his life to a young woman, and thought about looking it up and reading it to the press at the start of the walk through of the new exhibit. It was written by the artist in May 1937 and dealt with a group of ladies Parrish was expecting to come for a walk through of his own studio. She mused while smiling to the remembered words. Parrish had written:

> *"Today, these ladies were some literary guild I think they said and I dare say the majority could read and write. Tomorrow ten more are booked: organizers of Girl Scouts or the like, and you'll see me perched on my wood box at the usual matinee. It's quite an idea sitting on a sharp piece of stove wood: it gives you a pained expression which to them is interpreted as becoming shyness by this artist in the presence of so many and it helps in the fresh quality of my delivery.... And so it goes, it would not be so bad if at least once in a while there was one present who was worth looking at, but that kind don't run with the herd...."[1]*

She was sure the press would like it. Parrish had such a quiet, witty sense of humor.

When she got to her desk, she saw that she had been provided by the Board's Secretary with a copy for her files of the letter sent to Prudence Cartwright. She read it again and wondered how Prudence was going to take it. From what she remembered of her, even as a young intern working with her at the Boston Fine Arts Museum, she remembered that "Prudy" as she called her then, brooked no interference when she had her mind set to do something..."Oh, well! Let's hope she gets over the

---

[1] <u>Maxfield Parrish: The Secret Letters</u>. Gilbert, Alma. Alma Gilbert Books, San Pedro, CA 2012. P.72

disappointment and finds her prospective client another Parrish landscape, just not *Dingleton Farm!*" she mused.

Her phone rang and since there were still no staff members in yet, she answered it herself. "Margaret," the familiar cool voice of the board's President was on the other line. "Just heard from Prudence Cartwright's people saying she had received our letter declining to sell *Dingleton*, but that she had left the meeting early a few nights ago, and she had not seen your installation of the exhibit and is flying in today, to have a look."

"Samantha, today is the day for the Press Preview and as you know, we usually don't allow people to come see the exhibit before it opens to the public."

"Margaret, that's nonsense. Mrs. Cartwright gave us a generous donation a few nights ago that will help us meet the insurance cost of the museum owned pieces. I'm sure you'll see it in your heart to welcome her and walk her through the exhibit whenever she arrives. Where is your sense of duty as museum director? I told Mrs. Cartwright that there's no need to rent a car. I will meet her at the Lebanon airport, bring her to the museum, show her around, buy lunch perhaps at the Windsor Station Restaurant and then drive her back to catch the afternoon flight back to New York. She mentioned she might have another possible donor to the museum in mind and we can't squander that opportunity. Frankly, you sometimes give the impression that all the years you've worked here have gotten you set in your ways and not able to assimilate new ideas and methods. Remember you are long past your retirement date, dear.

Don't give me a reason to bring that delicate subject up with the board."

The implied threat was not lost on Maggie. She wadded a piece of paper where she had written a few notes to say to the reporters and threw it at the garbage can across the way and missed! Somehow, she would have to "suck it up" as her grandchildren said and try to be as welcoming as she could to the unexpected visitor.

CHAPTER TEN

Samantha Vanderpool's. sleek Mercedes AMG V-12
(perhaps not a good car to use in Vermont or New
Hampshire's rugged hills) roared up the museum's near
vertical hill, raising clouds of choking dust along the way
and deposited the two women at the entrance of the
main building. Already there were a number of cars in
the driveway including a couple of vans from the TV
stations WMUR and WCAX representing the twin states
media outlets.

The women went in and after a quick visit to the ladies
room, proceeded to go to the exhibit area where Maggie
was already conducting a walk through with the
reporters.

The group gathered around *Dingleton Farm* were busy
photographing the museum's newest addition. The
addition of the large Klieg lights for the TV stations
made the little painting glow, almost as if it knew it was
the center of attention.

Maggie was being asked by a young woman broadcaster
what she felt was the value of the new work and she

demurred politely saying that it was best not to publish values in the paper, but Yes, the painting had been added to the existing insurance policy at an appropriate value.. The museum's director noticed the newcomers and nodded in their direction, but continued her explanation of the theme of the exhibit and the importance of the works that had been gathered from different museums and individuals loaning them to the exhibition. At the end of the press preview, Maggie headed for where Samantha and Prudence were viewing other works on exhibit to welcome them.

"Quite a buzz you're creating with the addition of the new painting, isn't it, Maggie?" said Samantha in an attempt at mending fences with her museum director.

"Yes, the press seems quite taken by it and some of the more enterprising ones plan to continue up the way to New Hampshire and actually film the 150 year old farm with its iconic stone fence that Mr. Parrish depicted in the painting. Of course, they won't be able to reproduce the beautiful twilight glow that the work depicts." Then turning to Prudence Cartwright, she again thanked her for the generous donation which had allowed them to insure the painting in their portfolio of owned works.

"I was telling Mrs. Vanderpool that I have a very wealthy Chicago client that may be interested in also doing a substantial donation to the museum. May I bring him down to the Lender's and Donors party to which I have just been invited? I know he has not yet donated anything, but he could possible triple or quadruple my own donation if he likes what you're

69

showing and the mission of this small museum."

Samantha's eyes were glowing with anticipation and gave Maggie a look that said in effect: "See, this is how you raise money for the cause of the museum: by bringing in well heeled donors that can allow us to meet and pay our bills."

Maggie could not argue with the concept, so she tried her best to be accommodating and welcoming to Prudence Cartwright. Prudence had just shot her a look that bespoke volumes in saying how she had not forgotten that Maggie had in fact torpedoed her attempts to acquire the painting for her wealthy client, possibly now being represented as a well heeled "donor" who could help the museum with a sizable donation.

"I am impressed with the magnificent works that have been corralled for this exhibit", Prudence began, buttering up Samantha so she could get some of the information she had traveled to obtain. "They are very valuable. Is the museum adequately protected? What type of museum safety methods are you using to safeguard your treasures and those loaned by others? I may, perhaps lend you something from my galleries in the future and I would need to know how well they're protected."

Samantha could not wait to tell her what the alarm features were, where it was located, its maker, and how the doors and windows had also safety features that would sound if the alarm were triggered. "We also have a very special feature", she crowed. "Mrs. Winters tell me that in some of the very important works, a little button is attached to the back that is activated when the alarm is turned off, so if a painting were taken out of the building with its frame, it would re-activate the alarm and sound off."

"Interesting", responded Prudence. "I believe we have the same alarm system as yours in our galleries and have considered using the same button-on-the-frame feature ourselves, because as you may know, we also handle some very special and important works of art. They are not very bulky, are they?"

"Not at all", Samantha gushed. "Mrs. Winters tells me they're unobtrusive and are attached to the frame. Here. Let's ask her to show us one."

Maggie was not happy to reveal the safe feature of the little button, but seeing that Samantha was hovering possessively next to Prudence, she took a work down and showed them the back where the little unobtrusive blue button was affixed. "So that sets off the alarm even if it's not on if the work is carried out past the alarm panel next to the door?" Prudence asked innocently.

"Yes, Mrs. Cartwright. That will activate the special code set in each button and the alarm sounds even if it had been turned off if the painting goes out the door."

"Do all the paintings and art objects have that on?", queried Prudence "it must be beastly expensive!"

Maggie felt uncomfortable answering the question

because not all of the works had the special feature attached to them. Seeing the silence Samantha Vanderpool jumped in to assure Prudence. "The museum attaches that to all the important art objects loaned to us and I believe we should have that also attached to *Dingleton's* frame, don't you agree, Margaret?"

"I'm sure that can be arranged prior to the opening", answered Maggie. She didn't like conversing and divulging specific safety features carried by the museum. Prudence was desperate to inspect the back of the frame so she pressed on with her inquiries. "Is that one of Parrish's original frames in *Dingleton* now, would you be able to show me the back of it?"

Maggie replied "As you probably already know, Mr. Parrish created many of his own frames in his very well equipped studio. Most of the early frames were large black ones but in later years, he created lighter frames with a touch of blue at the center and a light touch of gold on the rim to use his favorite colors of blue and gold most people call the famous Parrish Blue. As you can see, this is one of those frames."

Eager to learn a new snippet about Parrish, Samantha quickly interjected. "I'm sure Margaret will be happy to show us the back of the frame."

After shooting her a look of displeasure, Maggie reluctantly acceded and took the beautiful little oil on board down and turned it over for their inspection. "It doesn't have the little button yet, does it?" Samantha pointed out.

"Not yet, but it will be soon done, Mrs. Vanderpool." Maggie answered without divulging that the work was going to be out of the exhibit space for a couple of weeks while it was being cleaned and varnished by Jeff.

In the meantime, Prudence on the pretext of interest in the museum and gallery labels affixed to the frame, carefully inspected it noting the manner and the type of butterfly screws Parrish had used to secure the painting to the frame. These were done so no harm would come to the work itself, as would be the case if nails were used to affix it to the frame. Since the work was done on board as was the artist's custom beginning in the early 20's all the way until the time of his death, it had no stretcher bars, so butterfly type of screws would make it easy for the artist, framer or a restorer to remove the board from the frame without having to undo bent nails affixed to stretcher bars.

Satisfied with the knowledge she had come seeking, Prudence was now ready to go back. She looked at her watch meaningfully and said: "Oh, dear! I had forgotten I had an important client coming in to the gallery this evening, perhaps I should go back and catch an earlier flight so I miss some of the end of the day traffic and get to the gallery before he arrives. Would you mind awfully if I skipped the lunch and have you drive me back to the airport, Samantha?

Somewhat disappointed with missing important time chatting up the self-styled "Purveyor to the Stars", Samantha of course agreed to drive her back to the airport after extracting the promise that she would be back for the Patron and Donors dinner shortly after the opening of the exhibit, and hopefully bringing the advertised special donor in tow.

Samantha Vanderpool would have been mighty disappointed seeing the "special client" Prudence was supposed to be meeting that evening. A quick call on her cell phone to Les Wonkrowski while she was waiting for her plane confirmed that he would pick her up at the airport and that a meeting had been set up with a "professional" for later that evening in the penthouse apartment.

The "professional" whom Les had talked about appeared, in Prudence Cartwright's eyes, to be some sort of low life that had been recruited from the workers in the New Jersey dock area. After meeting him, and giving him specific instructions on the type of alarm the museum had, which was similar to the one in her New York gallery, and specifically the importance of leaving the frame behind so as not to trigger the alarm on the way out, she entrusted him to Les and asked him to make him conversant in how to disarm the alarm from the outside, and what wires to disconnect so as not to trigger the main alarm system.

CHAPTER ELEVEN

Jeff Andrews was on duty at the museum the next day and could not wait to begin working on cleaning and varnishing the little *Dingleton*. He felt grateful that he was allowed to minister to a Parrish original. He ignored the threatening clouds that promised, according to the weather people last night, a veritable deluge that they said might even impact the height of the Connecticut River and make it over overflow its banks.

Since Jeff lived on the New Hampshire side of the river, he thought it prudent to drive to Claremont before going to work and pick up the little giclee reproduction of *Dingleton* that had been done based on the image that Jeff had taken earlier in the week of the little painting. Maggie had given him specific instructions that she wanted it done on canvas laid down and glued to a board similar to those that Parrish used, done so as to fit the exact measurements of *Dingleton's* original frame. Jeff had originally questioned her reason for doing this, since Parrish had not used canvas in his paintings since the 1910's. Maggie had explained the reason for it. She did not want anyone who knew Parrish's work well to mistake the giclee for the original work that was being

75

cleaned. Thus the reason for having the duplicate done on canvas laid down on board: so that it would fit snugly in the Parrish frame and let the professionals know that the original was being cleaned or photographed and thus a copy of it substituted during its absence. After all, when the museum opened to the public, the original oil would be back from cleaning and Jeff could have the giclee as a souvenir to take home and enjoy. Maggie knew that many auction houses provided giclees of the works they had sold as a small gift to the original owners, so the empty spaces on their walls would still bear a professionally looking reproduction to ease the owner's loss at the parting of works that perhaps had been in their families for generations.

Jeff admired the giclee when he picked it up. A faithful reproduction to the original work and of course it did not have the glow that made the Parrish works famous, but it would do while he was working on cleaning and varnishing the original prior to the museum's opening. Whistling, he showed up to work and noticed Maggie must already be at her office since the alarms were turned off. He went into the exhibit room picked up the original painting he was going to be working on, and took both the giclee and the original to his studio. In a matter of just a few minutes, he had removed the original, inserted the giclee in its place and hung it back on the museum wall while he worked preparing the original for its called for cleaning.

At lunchtime he showed Maggie the installed giclee and let her know the original was in his workroom upstairs.

"Be sure to lock it up in the safe when you close at night, Jeff," she said.

"Will do, Maggie! Not a bad giclee. After I install the original back here, would you mind if I took the copy home to remind me I had worked on the original?"

Since that was exactly what Maggie had had in mind, she said "That should be O.K. Jeff. You have certainly put in extra hours without compensation, so you should have the giclee as a token gift from the museum. What would we do without you?"

"Thanks, Maggie. You know how much the welfare of this museum means to me. As a token of my appreciation, I'll frame one of the photos that I have of that gorgeous rhododendron tree in full bloom outside of the museum that I took last summer."

"That would be great, Jeff! Maybe we could do a series of postcards with some of your beautiful photos of the museum's heritage garden plants in their full summer bloom to sell in the museum's gift store."

"I'd like that a lot, thanks, Maggie!" With this, both staff members parted each to go to their offices or work rooms where their 'to-do' list before opening day just two weeks away were getting rather unwieldy. The announcements of the museum opening exhibit were out. The large mailing that went to former visitors from all 50 states as well as donors and lenders had gone out, given the dedicated team of volunteers led by the vivacious teenager Connie who served as a motivator of enthusiasm for the many elders who also volunteered to stuff and stamp announcements every year. All the non-profits of the area depended on their loyal cadre of volunteers to compete with the public's attention and bring visitors, the life blood of non-profits in the area, through their doors.

At the end of the day, after ascertaining that Jeff Andrews had left for the night, it was Maggie's turn to see that all the lights were out and doors and windows secured before turning the alarm on and walking out the door. She went home to a light meal, a good book and an early bedtime after a glass of sherry.

The peaceful feeling of the surroundings could not ever have presaged that her life was shortly about to be turned a complete 180 degrees and not necessarily in a happy way.

Early the next morning, a frantic ringing coming from her purse assaulted Maggie as she was getting in her trusty Subaru in preparation for the ride to the museum. She opened the car's door and rummaged through the clutter in her purse until she felt the smooth case of her little cell phone. She pulled it out and uncertain as to what to do, she managed to locate the ON button and instantly Jeff's distraught and almost screaming voice was shouting in her ear.

"Maggie! I just walked in and turned off the alarm which you set last night. THE ALARM WAS ON!!! (Well, of course, it was thought Maggie, I set it myself.) You don't understand, Maggie! Despite the fact that the

78

alarm was on, someone's been in the museum last night or this morning. *Dingleton's* frame was on the ground and it was EMPTY!" It took a few seconds for Maggie to interpret the information.

"But Jeff," she said, catching a little of his panic, "*Dingleton* wasn't in that frame last night. You put the giclee there and took the painting to your office to work on it. You probably stored the painting in the museum's vault last night before going home. DIDN'T YOU?" All of a sudden, Maggie had gone cold all over and started to tremble uncontrollably.

There was a brief moment of silence and then a voice with a small modicum of calm spoke again. "But of course, I did. I'm such an idiot! *Dingleton* should still be in the vault. I had just begun was working on it yesterday. Sorry, Maggie! When I saw the empty frame on the floor I totally panicked and my head went into reverse mode."

"That still does not tell us why the alarm was on and why the empty frame was on the floor, Jeff. I'll be there in three or four more minutes. Hold off and don't call the police until I get there." Maggie sped up the hill, the Subaru's motor complaining mightily with this uncalled for behavior from its owner. The museum's door was still open from when Jeff had entered and turned off the alarm as he did every morning when he came in ahead of the director. Jeff was still in the exhibit room looking at the empty frame on the floor and unable and unwilling to pick it up.

"This is how I found it, Maggie" he said pointing unnecessarily at the empty frame lying forlornly before its former space on the museum wall.

"Did you touch it at all, Jeff?"

"Not today, Maggie, but my prints must be all over the frame since I put the giclee in yesterday morning."

"Run upstairs, Jeff and check if the original is in the vault where you left it. Hurry! I need to call the police." Jeff took the stairs two or three steps at a time with his long legs, something that Maggie would never have been able to do. Within two or three minutes he was back cradling the little original in his hands and beaming widely."

"It's here, Maggie! It's safe!"

"Put it back in the safe, Jeff and leave it there until the police arrive." Hurriedly, she looked the police number upstairs in her office and called their barracks in the Windsor office about five or ten miles away.

Within minutes, the police followed by a Vermont trooper in his official car, pulled up before the museum and the sound of their boots on the parquet floor echoed loudly through the still empty museum. Maggie hurried down to meet them. She was well known by the deputy the police had sent since this was part of his territory beat, and he introduced her to the Vermont trooper, who tipped his hat to her silently and proceeded directly into the empty display room with the forlorn empty frame on the floor.

After ascertaining the pertinent data of who had found it and if the frame had been touched, they asked the important question: "Since it was a Parrish oil that was taken, what would be its approximate value, Maggie?"

"Thank God, the Parrish oil is safe. It was being cleaned and varnished upstairs by our restorer, Jeff Andrews. So when he left last night, it was put into the safe overnight. He didn't want to leave it out on his work table."

"Very wise, of him, Maggie but what was taken and you say the alarm was ON?" said Mike Walters, the policeman who responded to the call.

"Someone took the copy of *Dingleton* we made in Claremont while the painting was being cleaned. We have so many volunteers and journalists who want to take a quick look at the work for their articles, that after opening the exhibit to the press preview, we installed a copy in its frame so the exhibit would appear complete while Jeff finished the cleaning and varnishing of the work which will take three or four more days to complete."

"Why was the alarm still on? Did the intruder disarm it? And then when he left turned it back on? How would he know the code unless it was someone working in the museum?" the Vermont trooper wanted to know and then added a second thought: "How many staff members are privy to the code, Maggie?"

"Just Jeff and I" said Maggie thoughtfully and then, added: "Oh, the president of the museum's board of directors, Samantha Vanderpool also knows the code, but to our knowledge, she's never been called to set the alarm or turn it off. Every incoming president is given the new code which changes with each incoming administration."

And then she added, knowing what his next question would be, "I set it myself last night when I let myself out."

The Vermont trooper, snapped on a pair of rubber gloves and picked up the frame gingerly. "That is strange, isn't it? Who would skillfully break in without affecting the alarm and take a copy of a painting for his troubles?"

"Probably someone who was not bright or knowledgeable enough to tell the difference between a copy and an original, officer. The copy was a skillful giclee, the closest thing to an original and hard to distinguish unless you're thoroughly familiar with the painter's work."

"Someone's sure going to be surprised when they get back to whoever ordered the painted hoisted!" The trooper could not hide a little smile appearing behind his tough and professional veneer.

CHAPTER TWELVE

The Vermont trooper's idea that whoever had ordered the painting hoisted would be "surprised" when they received the giclee had not used quite the right word.

"Surprised" was not the word a fly on the wall would have heard if flies could hear. "Flabbergasted," "Venomous" or probably "Murderously Angry" would have been progressively closer to the mark.

After tearing open the foam padded wrap paper which Les had provided his "professional", and seeing what had been brought back from the heist, Prudence flung the giclee at the messenger who was standing idly by, catching him totally by surprise. The little canvas covered board hit him just above the eye, and opened a gash that immediately started to bleed.

"Stupid, idiotic jerk! That's not an original. That's a copy. Where's the original I saw hanging on the wall at the museum two days ago?"

You could see the "professional" narrowing his eyes and attempting to control his desire to bring out his gun and shoot the madwoman down. "Just wait one damn minute! You hired me because of my savvy with all kinds of alarms to drive to Vermont, disarm the museum's alarm before entering, go to the main exhibit, pick up a painting labeled *Dingleton Farm* hanging on the wall, leave the frame behind so that it would not trigger the alarm once I connected it again, and bring the painting on board to you. That was my job and that's what got done. Give me my fee. I'm done here!"

 "Like hell you are! " shouted Prudence and if the Lester had not held her back, she would have jumped and attached the "professional" with her manicured talons that looked murderous enough to cause serious damage to anyone's eyes. "I paid you to bring me back a painting, not a copy of a copy mounted on canvas! That's what I wanted and that's when you will get paid, you stupid bastard!"

 "STOP it Prudence! This won't get us anywhere. It looks as if the museum, for some reason or other, substituted the original you saw for this, whatever you call it, fake copy of the painting you wanted brought back. Maybe they were cleaning it, or took it to show to experts. Who knows? What will happen is this will have to be finessed better or else your client in Chicago is going to take out on us."

 "Trouble is" continued Les still holding Prudence who was struggling to get away from his iron grip, "They will be on the alert that someone tried to stead their precious painting and may take more rigorous measures to safeguard it. We'll need Vito's help again if he's to

84

attempt to take it once more, once they put the real painting back on the wall. Which they will have to do when it's being showed to the public or to their precious lenders and donors. They wouldn't dare put up a fake that could be examined by people who know their stuff. If I were them, I'd put it in their mammoth vault at nights and that would be infinitely more difficult to break into than just an alarm. That would keep it relatively safe from us", he said smiling sardonically at his own pun.

"I won't pay that low life until the real thing is brought back," hissed Prudence between her teeth while she still struggled to free herself from Lester's grip.

"Calm down, I'll take care of it with Vito. We'll need him again to pick up the real thing and besides, alarm experts who work under the radar are hard to find." With a nod from his head, Les wordlessly indicated to Vito that his presence was no longer needed.

"Come see me tomorrow and I'll take care of you." said Les. The alarm specialist, after shooting a long and murderous look at Prudence Cartwright, went out slamming the penthouse's entry door.

Les released his grip on Prudence and she stumbled back into a silk settee behind her. "Don't ever speak to my men or people I hire like that, they may turn against you when you least expect it, " he warned her his voice cold and venomous. "You do your job, and I'll do mine."

Prudence's mind was already racing, thinking of what might be the next good opportunity to try to acquire the painting again for her Chicago client.

"All right! I'll call my client tomorrow and tell him we have a small, unexpected delay in the delivery of his painting. He's going to be mad as hell, but I think I can stall him by asking him to come with me as a prospective donor to the museum's Patron and Donor Tea that's followed by a private showing of the exhibit before it opens to the public the next day. The showing will be followed by a dinner and that might present an opportunity for the painting to be acquired by your so-called expert while everyone's occupied."

"That's better. Now you're thinking, " was Lester's only comment before walking out of the penthouse without a backwards look at the art dealer who still lay half reclined, half sitting on the settee.

The next morning in New York dawned grey and misting a little, which would complicate the work commute. By eight Prudence had already put in a call to Chicago and talked with her client. Of course, he was apoplectic that the painting he was expecting had not yet materialized.

"Tell your 'Expediter' to get the job done or else I'll do it with my own people and you won't get crap out of this deal. Why should I pay you if I can have my own people bring it in for me? I now know where the painting is. Easy pickings for a real professional."

Prudence convinced him to wait a week longer and suggested he might enjoy seeing the work hanging among its peers in the exhibit before it was "delivered" to him. The novelty of the idea must have appealed to the gruff sounding man on the phone. He said to make arrangements and call him back with details of where to meet before the event so they would arrive together. He exhorted her that he was not a patient man.

Relieved, Prudence proceeded to set the stage for the event. She called the president of the museum board and convinced her that a very powerful and moneyed donor would be interested in perhaps giving a substantial donation to a museum which specialized on the works of the important artists of the American Cornish Colony and would be interested in seeing a collection of the groups painting and sculptures in one single place.

Samantha Vanderpool asked for his name and address to send an immediate invitation but Prudence demurred and said he preferred to remain anonymous but would attend the opening with her and Mr. Wonkrowski if Samantha were to send her an extra invitation to the gala affair. The president of the board accepted with alacrity and promised to send an overnight envelope with their invitations to Samantha's gallery in Chicago.

Prudence was gleeful that the stage was set and since she would be present, there would be little chance of her plans going wrong the second time around.

Meanwhile, it had been decided with the consensus of the board members that since nothing of value had been taken, no further action or claim would result from the obvious break-in at the museum. The Treasurer of the board had counseled that there should be no leak to the press of the break-in because that would make their insurance carrier nervous and might result in a sudden spike in their premiums and the Risk Level designation.

It was also decided by the board that it should expand to two more members, still leaving an odd number so that all votes should not have to suffer a tie. Two new names were added for consideration, one candidate from New Hampshire and one from Vermont: James Duncan, a retired art history professor from Dartmouth College in Hanover and Ronnie Santini, an Italian restaurateur from one of the better restaurants in Windsor, Vermont. Both men were well known to the board because they served often as museum volunteers and docents. James was often called by Maggie and usually consulted on troublesome art history conundrums and Ronnie had been the caterer of choice for their many functions. It was time that their expertise and knowledge of their subjects and the community they lived in be tapped by the museum to serve on their board.

The men were contacted on the spot while the board was still present at the emergency meeting Maggie had requested to inform everyone of the troubling break-in the night before. To Maggie's relief, they both accepted and promised to drop by the museum during the week before the opening to consult with the director and board president and be given a copy of the board's manual and meeting minutes.

On the day following the emergency board meeting, Maggie and Jeff had decided that for the time being, the empty frame would be brought upstairs and at the end of the day after Jeff finished working on the cleaning and varnishing, the painting would be stored within the big walk in safe in the evenings, instead of being allowed to remain on Jeff's work easel as was sometimes the case when he was working on cleaning or restoration.

She was grateful that some of her best friends in the area were now members of the board. She breathed a sigh of relief knowing that she would have their advice and friendship on her side. She felt warm and cosseted in the embrace and trust of their friendship. It was also nice to have people she trusted implicitly circulating as part of the board and keeping eyes and ears open during the upcoming convocation of trustees, donors and contributors to the exhibit.

After a hectic week of final preparations, it seemed that the month of May had finally broken Mother Nature's mood and the museum and its staff were busy putting the final touches before the important Lenders and Donors exhibit opened ahead of the general opening the following Monday. The grounds were spiffy and the spirea, rhododendrons, peonies and the century old lilacs were blooming, their perfume spilling in the air. The magnificent pines and two and three hundred year oak trees dotting the gardens around the museum, provided welcome respite of shade for the workers in the garden. Denny had used some of the museum's maintenance budget to make sure that the hill's winter damage had been repaired and all the ruts filled in. Maggie had splurged and ordered that the windows of the hundred year old grand mansion that housed the museum be washed professionally and its parquet floors shined.

Jeff had finished the cleaning, varnishing and drying of the little *Dingleton*. It had now taken its place in the exhibit walls along with the other paintings. The staff had scurried making sure the lights shone directly upon the paintings that were being shown as well as the sculptures in the middle of the salons. The caterers from Ronnie Santini's establishment were scurrying about unloading the van carrying pre dinner goodies as well as the dinner which would be later warmed in the house's century old kitchen that a past owner had refurbished and modernized enough to hold appliances equivalent to good kitchens from the fifties or sixties.

Maggie left the museum a little after three to go to her cottage for a quick shower and a change to evening wear. She returned in time to allow Jeff to also change into his dress pants and shirt that he had brought with him, since his home was across the river.

Maggie went into the room that had been set aside for the initial tea. The museum's volunteers were responsible for most of the preparations: the trays of delicious pastries and the different teas that were being served and poured from hundred year old silver servers polished to a high degree of gloss for this function every year. Many of the New Englanders attending preferred natural herbal teas, but the traditional array of Earl Grey and other prepared teas were also available. Jeff, an inveterate tea drinker had brought a special concoction of his own and placed it in a small silver dispenser where he knew it would be available to him.

Shortly before six, cars' headlights made their way up the hill with board members and the first of the early invitees. The president of the board, the vice-president, and treasurer formed a welcoming committee and greeted arrivals at the door and provided them with the prepared name tags. The ladies wore long dresses. The men were in dinner jackets and dark trousers. Prudence Cartwright arrived with Les Wonkrowski and a portly gentleman in tow. Since the art dealer had not provided a name for her guest, a blank nametag was ready. Hesitating briefly as if he were debating whether to give his real name or not, he hastily scrawled "Mr. Jones" on the tag and told Samantha Vanderpool that he preferred not to give his surname which he said was unpronounceable any way. Understanding his need for privacy if he was, as Prudence had described, a possible large donor, Samantha smiled knowingly and made her best effort to make him feel welcome, whoever he really was.

Guests were first led to where the formal tea had been set. To accommodate the tastes of some of the gentlemen attending, Maggie had also set up a liquor bar that was much appreciated, especially by some of the male donors. Samantha had announced to the guests that tea and cocktails were being served until seven when the guests would then tour the new exhibit areas that were presently locked. Dinner would be served promptly at eight in the house's dining room that housed a twenty-foot long formal table which had come with the house when it had been acquired by the museum.

"Your director is getting a little long in the tooth", whispered Prudence cattily to Samantha as they entered the room where the volunteers had begun to pour tea and pass plates for the delicacies around the table, "when are you going to get new blood in here to direct the exhibits? I have several acquaintances in New York with young people who have trained for art history degrees in the best colleges. When you finally realize that you need someone younger and a little more flexible let me know, I'd be happy to give you some recommendations."

"Yes, I've thought the time is getting right for her to retire and I plan to speak privately to the board and make that recommendation very soon," Samantha agreed with her. "I would appreciate knowing who's available out there."

"I'll get back to you on that", smiled Prudence with a glint of malice in her eyes.

Jeff, who had been helping man the cocktail table, could not help overhearing the conversation of the two women. He turned the duty over to James Duncan the new board member and angled his way to where saw Prudence eyeing critically the array of tea selections. The museum staff including Maggie, her secretary, and Jeff were on duty in the room where the tea had been set. The director was filling teacups and passing them to the incoming guests. She offered Prudence some, who tasted it and immediately put her cup down. "Don't they have a good strong tea available?" she asked Jeff critically.

"Well, I always bring my own special blend, but it's not for the weak of heart. I make it myself and it contains several herbal and flower petals, including a few of the rhododendron and azalea leaves of the bush outside the museum, but not too many of those," he added hastily. "I usually don't share it, but I would be happy to give you a taste of it if you wish to see if you like it. I prefer to serve it with a honey that's made locally."

"Well, I'll try it and see if it's better than the rest of this insipid lot of store bought tea bags," was the haughty reply.

Jeff located the small silver decanter that contained the tea he had brought in and poured her a cup. He placed it in a small silver tray along with a jar of the special honey he had brought and offered it to the art dealer. "Enjoy," he said and then left and went back to relieve James behind the cocktail table.

Prudence took a sip or two and making a face, left the cup on the table where the dishes were being stacked and proceeded to join a line at the cocktail table where the Les and Mr. Jones were being served what was obviously not their first martini.

Promptly at seven, the table chimes were rung announcing to the assembled guests that the exhibit doors had been rolled back making the room ready for their entrance.

By twos and threes the group entered through the double carved doors that led to one of the three exhibit spaces part of which at one time had been the first owner's library. Maggie was delighted to hear the "Oh's" and "Ah's" of the assembled group as they inspected the assembled collection and carefully read the printed labels, which identified not only the name of the work, its creator, size, year and date but also the name of the lender or donor. After all, this is what this assembled group was here to see and celebrate.

Mr. Jones followed closely by Prudence and Les seemed quite taken by *Dingleton Farm*. Imperceptibly, he nodded his satisfaction to Prudence who smiled broadly. "I knew you'd like it! Now please make noises to the president of the board about being interested in making a donation to the museum, so she sees you as a big shot she needs to impress." was her savvy request.

Prudence was pleased that the client from Chicago was quite taken with the work. She and Les would see to it that they helped him make that acquisition. She took Les aside and whispered. "Is Vito ready to get this when everybody is out of here and sitting down to dinner? They'll probably lock the doors of the exhibit space again but can't turn on the alarms until all of us are out of the building at the end of the dinner."

"Locks and alarms are no problem to Vito, " whispered Les back to her. "By the way, you're perspiring all over. You O.K? It's not that hot here. Your make-up is beginning to run", he added critically.

"I didn't know women's make-up was also part of your expertise, Les," Prudence snapped cattily. "But then again, maybe there's things about you that you don't like others to know." Lester's narrowed eyes flashed a warning. "Maybe you don't know when to shut up," he hissed brutally.

The room WAS definitely too warm in Prudence's estimation. She was also beginning to feel a little clammy and her stomach was churning as if she were ready to vomit. "I need some air, here!" she told herself and made a hasty albeit tottery exit on her high-heeled dress shoes and headed straight for the door that opened out to the fragrant garden. She looked frantically towards her car. Maybe her blood pressure was acting up. She needed to take her pills. She spotted her car and headed towards it, but didn't make it. She felt the blow strike her and mercifully, she slumped in a heap, her hand still outstretched towards the door of her Mercedes.

Inside, the discreet dinner chimes were rung and the guests led by the President of the board, now firmly at the arm of Mr. Jones, headed for the formal dining room.

After ascertaining that the guests had all left the exhibit rooms, Maggie and Jeff prepared to close and lock the doors. "I'll turn off the lights, and lock up, Maggie. We won't turn on the alarms until everyone has left the building at the end of the dinner. You go ahead with your guests. I'll be in in a few minutes as soon as I lock up."

"Thanks, Jeff. I'd best see if the caterers are all right and if they have begun serving" Maggie agreed gratefully and hurried past where the people were finding their name place cards and taking their seats. Seemingly all was in order with the caterers, so after a quick look to see if the volunteers had cleaned and closed the reception area where the tea had been held, she took her place between two board members, Bert Lincoln and the newest inductee to the board, retired Dartmouth art history professor, James Duncan. She looked around to see if Jeff had made it to the table and not seeing him or Prudence at their assigned seats, she started to rise when Bert held her hand and said, "Relax, Maggie. It's time you enjoyed a little of what you have set up. Here comes the first course."

Maggie agreed and sat down to enjoy the delicious cold soup that the caterer's had chosen for the first course. Eventually she noted with relief that Jeff had joined the diners and was sitting next to an elderly lady donor who was delighted that her dinner companion was such a comparatively young and pleasant member of the museum staff.

She looked around and noted that neither Prudence nor Lester had been seated. Mr. Jones was being monopolized by Samantha and seemed content to be so treated. Prudence was still nowhere in sight.

The second course was in the process of being served when Les Wonkrowski burst into the room and said without preamble: "Has anyone seen Mrs. Cartwright? I don't think she was feeling well and may have wandered off to get some air. She's not in the museum or the ladies room".

"I'll go looking for her", said Maggie rising promptly from her chair. "I'll come with you," piped Bert pushing his plate aside and, winking his eye, playfully instructed James Duncan, "Don't you dare eat my steak when it comes in, Jim!"

One of the first doors they tried was the exhibit rooms, but of course, they were securely locked. Maggie looked in the ladies room downstairs and Bert took a quick survey of the floors above. Nothing seemed amiss and there was no one up there. "Is her car still outside?" The two were headed out when suddenly the portly figure of Denny, their grounds keeper, burst through the front doors.

"Better call an ambulance, Maggie. There's a woman collapsed outside by a Mercedes and I can't feel a pulse!"

Maggie looked stunned and was just headed for her office to call when she noticed that Bert Lincoln was stabbing his cell phone with his fingers and asking the 911 operator to send an ambulance to the museum on River Road. The three then rushed out, led to the spot by Denny. The crumpled form of Prudence Cartwright lay on the ground, the keys to her car still clutched in her right hand. Bert felt for a pulse and could not detect one. The clammy face seemed contorted and her eyes were open but unseeing. "She's gone, Maggie!" The words sounded so ominous as he said them.

ALMA GILBERT

CHAPTER THIRTEEN

The wail of the ambulance could already be heard coming up River Road. The red lights of the approaching vehicle were casting ominous shadows against the tall trees. Upon its arrival, three emergency technicians rushed to where people had begun to congregate, including Bert and Denny who flanked Maggie side by side, whispering and watching the prone figure on the ground. Briskly, the EMT techs dropped their equipment next to the body and asked to have people return to the building. Everyone complied except Maggie, Bert and Denny. The body's vital signs were checked and a defibrillator called for. The body shook and trembled under the voltage, but remained inert afterwards. The technicians attempted resuscitation and mouth to mouth with no avail. Finally, shaking their heads, they covered the body and loaded it in the waiting ambulance.

"Do we have the woman's name and does she have family nearby we could notify?" one of the technicians asked Maggie, whom they knew as director of the museum.

"Her name is…was", she corrected herself, "Prudence Cartwright, a visitor from New York. She's here with an associate and a client that may want to speak to you before you remove the body."

Les Wonkrowski had made his way outside despite the entreaties of some of the board members and elbowed his way past Denny, who was trying to keep the area clear for the EMT people to work.

"What's wrong with her? She's with me. She's my employer. She seemed a little ill inside and must have come out for some fresh air."

"She's dead, sir. May I have your name and that of a close relative we could contact?" the female EMT queried, looking at him and appraising his seemingly cool reaction at the news of Prudence's death.

"Les Wonkrowski. I'm Mrs. Cartwright's associate." Strangely, he did not seem surprised to see the covered pallet already loaded in the ambulance. He spelled out his name for her. "She has a couple of adult kids in Chicago. The office there would have that information. She's also got a daughter in California but I don't have her address or number. Here's our card. You can call them on Monday. Doubt there will be anyone there tonight or Sunday."

The EMT tech closed her laptop and got into the ambulance which turned around and left the parking area with its red and amber lights on, but had silenced the sirens. It made its way gingerly down the hill, carrying the body of the Chicago gallery owner. A waiting Vermont police car let them negotiate the hill, before proceeding up themselves. The younger police officer driving the car turned to Officer Mike Walters, his superior and commented. "Guess they're no longer in a hurry. Their siren is silenced. Must mean the body could not be resuscitated and they're taking it to the morgue instead of the hospital."

"The medical examiner has to examine the body first and issue a preliminary cause of death before the morgue gets it for delivery to the next of kin" was Officer Walters laconic answer to the newer man. "Here in Vermont, we don't have nearly the number of sudden deaths that the big cities have, so it's not as if the medical examiner is swamped with requests for his time. If he has any question or suspicions, he refers them to the pathologist up at Dartmouth Hospital for back up and post mortem. Let's see what Maggie Winters can tell us about the person so we can file a report."

The officers parked their patrol car and made their way to where a knot of people made up of Maggie, Bert, Denny, Mr. Jones and Les had stayed since they were at the site where the body had been found.

"Hiya, Maggie, Bert, Denny. What do we have here? Seems I was just here a few days ago investigating a possible theft, which thank God you felt had not been a loss of any amount of value, right?"

"Just a print, Mike. But you're right about the value. There's another more important sounding name for a good print, but that doesn't change its worth."

Officer Walters took out his pad and began writing the details of the call while his driver held the flashlight so that he could see since the parking area was not that well lit. With the suddenness of a lightning strike, the air was rendered apart by a scream from the museum area. In a moment, the distraught figure of Samantha Vanderpool came rushing past the few spectators gathered near the entryway to watch the police and ambulance vehicles arriving and departing. Pushing people to the side she headed straight for where the police car and its little knot of people being interviewed were standing.

"Are the police here, Margaret?", she cried unnecessarily, seemingly without noticing Officer Walters standing in front of her taking the report from the museum director.

"We're the ones in uniform, lady!" was Mike Walters' laconic answer. He was not very tolerant of the pushy outsiders who came in from other states thinking that their money gave them a certain elevated status among established Vermonters.

"*DINGLETON* IS MISSING!!!" Samantha wailed.

Mike Walters pushed his iconic Vermont police trooper hat a little higher on his forehead so that she could see that he was not at all pleased at the news. "Missing again, is it?" was his only comment.

Maggie and Bert's reactions were identical. They looked

at each other and ran towards the museum. They found the door to the exhibit room, which Jeff had supposedly locked before coming to sit down to dinner, opened wide and the empty frame of the painting, seemingly hung as a mocking gesture, in its rightful place on the museum wall, its precious contents gone.

"It was here just an hour ago when Jeff locked the room down before joining us at the banquet table", wailed Maggie, her numb mind unable to process the grotesque sight of an empty frame, hanging forlornly on the museum wall without its inner treasure. She reached for it and was held back by both Bert and Mike Walters.

"Don't touch the frame, Maggie. We need to see whose prints are there", Mike quickly warned.

"Obviously mine and Jeff's since we hung it there", said Maggie and then followed immediately by a thought that stabbed her psyche. "Where's Jeff? Please find him!!"

The Vermont trooper drew a pair of rubber gloves from one of his pockets and picked up the frame gingerly. "What's this little button in the back? Is that connected to the alarm at all?" Maggie nodded her assent dumbly and then asked if she could go find Jeff. "It's not activated unless the painting and its frame leaves the building. Then it triggers automatically and makes the alarm sound even if it's not turned on as would be the case now while people are still in the premises."

The trooper nodded silently while he radioed in to headquarters that he had a possible high end theft in progress and to send the nearest available backup patrol car so that no one would either go up or down the hill until he had talked to them.

Denny volunteered to park his truck obstructing the entrance to the hill until the patrol car arrived and was nodded into action by the trooper. Maggie and Bert took the stairs two by two, calling Jeff's name, but their calls were met by silence in the dark upstairs where the offices and working areas of the museum were located.

CHAPTER FOURTEEN

In the meantime, the assembled guests, donors, lenders and other distinguished dignitaries that had been present were milling aimlessly between the dining room and the room where the tea had been served, which were the only rooms other than the kitchen where the lights were on. Many were on their cell phones including Les and the Mr. Jones, both with backs turned away making whispered comments to unknown recipients on the other end.

Maggie called out from the top of the stairs. "Is Jeff Andrews downstairs?"

"Doesn't seem to be Maggie!", a couple of her staff or board members answered.

In the meantime, Bert who was as familiar with the museum layout as any of the staff members was systematically going room to room and flipping light switches on to the different staff and work rooms, calling out Jeff's name as he opened the doors.

There was a sudden silence to his voice, and Maggie

came out to the hall where she had also been going from room to room in the opposite direction.

"Maggie, in here. I've found him!" Maggie rushed to the room where Bert was standing just outside of the door but he blocked her way. "Bring Mike Walters up here, Maggie. Quickly!", he said to distract her momentarily.

Maggie leaned over the ornate balustrade of the stairway and called out for the Trooper. He came up taking the steps by three's in quick order and entered the room.

"Wait here, Maggie, please!" Bert's voice entreated her at the same time blocking her view of Jeff's work area. "It's not a pretty sight". And saying this, he held her firmly against his chest, still preventing her from looking into the room.

"Holy Mother of God!" Mike Walters spoke out loud. Then realizing that the museum director was just standing outside the door, he came out and gently closed the door behind him. "We're going to treat this as a crime room, Maggie, so until the police photographer can come in and have people from the crime scenes clear the room, no one is going to be allowed in."

"Jeff...?"

"He's gone, Maggie, we can't help him now except by catching whoever did this to him", said the Vermont trooper solemnly

Maggie began trembling uncontrollably and seeing this, Bert went to her side and brought her shaking body next to his. He held her tightly, silently willing her to stop her natural protest about the happenings all around, providing a steady calming influence to her shaken psyche.

Mike saw the shaken elderly director being held and came over to them. "If it's any consolation to you, Maggie, it was fast and Jeff probably had no time to react."

"But how, Mike, who could have done all…all of this? Prudence Cartwright, the painting, and now our dear Jeff.?" Maggie was usually a strong woman who prided herself in crying very seldom, but all of a sudden, unbidden tears came crowding into her eyes, spilling silently down her cheeks.

She was suddenly conscious that the front of Bert's white shirt was wet with her tears, and she pulled away, trying vainly to stop the heaving of her chest and those unbidden tears. Drawing an immaculate handkerchief from his trouser's pocket, Bert silently offered it to Maggie who first dried her face and then tried vainly to mop up his tear stained shirt.

"Oh, Bert! I'm so sorry! I've ruined your good shirt."

"You've done nothing of the kind, Maggie. The dry cleaners will take care of this in short order."

While they were speaking a new patrol car stopped at the museum's front entrance and two or three lab people joined the police already there and were both pointed upstairs to Jeff's former workroom, as well as to the main museum's exhibit area which had been guarded by Mike Walters' rookie police driver. The crime lab people had brought in their white crime scene suits, donned them and entered the room, closing the door behind them and began assessing and photographing the scene, the position of Jeff's body and the blood spatters on the wall.

They quickly determined that Jeff, had been almost guillotined by a sharp object. The medical examiner entered, knelt to examine the position of the body, the knife cut, took several photos and then covered the body and asked for a gurney to take it downstairs and into the waiting ambulance.

In the meantime, Mike Walters and his young rookie had rounded up the approximately twenty donors, guests and board members and were efficiently taking names and addresses for interrogation purposes. Many of the donors and lenders were from out of state, so they were instructed to stay in the area at least until Monday to allow for the police interviews to take place.

CHAPTER FIFTEEN

Most of the guests were shocked and saddened at the horrific end of what had promised to be a renaissance for the new museum with its ambitious exhibit. Most accepted willingly and gave the names of their hotels or inns where they were staying locally. Mike Walters promised to complete their interviews first, ahead of those people who lived locally. He had also instructed his men to be aware, while they were taking the initial information of names, reason for attendance and places where they could be contacted over the weekend, if there were anyone whose clothes might show either spatters of blood or some other semblance of a struggle.

Many of the attendees had already been at their cell phones informing family or businesses about their probable delay in getting back. Members of the board were scurrying about trying to be of help to the police but they were told politely to stay together if possible in one room for their initial interrogation. The police were interested in having their version on what may have happened, where they were at the time of the occurrences and other important factors relevant to finding out what had occurred and in unraveling stories and time frames that might conflict with each other.

It was not until well after midnight that the last car left the area and hurried down the hill towards either homes or to the hotels and inns where out of town guests were spending the night. The first to leave had been Mr. Jones along with Lester, who had both been glued to their phones from the time the police arrived until they were asked for their information and allowed to depart with the promise that they would be available for a more detailed interview the next day. Since they had come together in Prudence Cartwright's car, Les had a duplicate set of keys which he now used to drive the client from Chicago to the famous French Inn and Restaurant across the river in New Hampshire where he had been booked for the night.

Samantha Vanderpool had instructed Maggie and the members of the board to meet at the museum on Monday after their depositions had been given to the police to assess the damage and what could and would be said to the press when they found out. Some enterprising members of the different newspapers, radio and TV stations had already been aware of the lights and the commotion visible for miles around since the museum was located on a hill near the Connecticut River and its lights could be seen from both adjacent areas in Vermont and across the river in New Hampshire. The museum's phone lines were lit and clamoring for attention, but had gone unanswered.

The board's preliminary idea was that a press release from Maggie would be sent out announcing a delay in the opening day activities the following week the very next morning. Maggie and Bert were the last to leave the museum, turn off the lights and set the alarm one more time….so much had transpired since the last evening, when dear Jeff had been the last to leave to allow Maggie a little more time to prepare and dress for this opening event. Bert walked Maggie to her car and hugged her once. As he handed her into the Subaru, he leaned on her driver's window and whispered: "COURAGE!!" before closing her door and patting the car in a gesture of luck.

 Still numb with the shock of the events, Maggie's mind just would not accept the horrific developments. Automatically, she pulled into her little cottage's driveway and leaving her headlights on until she could locate her door keys, she approached the path surrounded and enveloped by the silence of a country evening. She opened the door, located the switch for her entryway light and hurried to turn off her headlights before she wasted any more of the battery. She entered what for many years she saw as her sanctuary after a trying day, tossed her bag aside and promptly kicked off her heels. Before making herself comfortable, she turned the heat on her kitchen stove and began warming the water in her kettle for a very needed cup of chamomile tea.

 While waiting for the kettle, she was standing in the front room, flexing her aching soles, when all of a sudden a rush of wind slammed her front door closed making her jump and causing her hands to begin trembling unbidden. She hurried and turned on all the lights to make sure there were no unwanted intruders like a stray raccoon or possum which sometimes found their way to her larder if she left the front door open a few minutes for ventilation. Finding no critters on sight, she sank into her couch strategically placed in front of her little stone fireplace and which gave her a great deal of comfort at the end of a long day. She threw a log on the supports and expertly started a little fire in its hearth. Soon, the room would be filled with its warmth.

Her mind wandered and reviewed step by step all the details of the evening's happenings, trying to make sense of them. She was aware of the complete silence of the room with the exception of the ticking of her mother's Seth Thomas grandfather clock that stood as a silent guardian over her at the corner of the room and thought of Maxfield Parrish's words on a letter he had written to a young woman with whom he had fallen deeply in love late in his life.

"*The kettle is on for tea: a ruby fire is half talking to itself, and it is so silent here that the clocks ticks sound like hammer blows.*"[2]

"Some things don't seem to change, around here, do they, Mr. Parrish?" Maggie thought addressing the

---

[2] Maxfield Parrish: The Secret Letters. Gilbert, Alma. p. 51. Alma Gilbert Books, San Pedro, CA. 2012

deceased artist with whom she felt such a kindred spirit, caring for and loving his works so much…."Wonder what he thinks of this theft?", she asked herself. Luckily no one knew of this long standing habit of Maggie's and her silent "conversations" with her favorite artist.

Her teakettle and phone chose that precise moment to go off together. Grabbing her purse and trying to locate her cell phone at the same time she hurried to get the kettle off the stove. Seeing that it was Bert's number, she answered it breathlessly as she put the kettle down.

"You sound as if you've been running, Maggie. You O.K.?" the comforting gruff voice of her friend said.

"O.K. for the state I'm in, I guess, Bert. Just hurrying to get the tea kettle off the stove. Making myself a cup of chamomile."

"Good idea! Works better if you put a little brandy in it to help you sleep and relax after the day you've had! Just called because after driving a little way towards home and passing your house, I noticed there was a car parked there on the side of the entry road and at this time of the night and with all what's going on, just wanted to see that you were O.K."

Maggie felt a prickle of fear at the back of her neck, but she dismissed it, shaking her head. "Everything is quiet here, Jeff. I didn't see any cars when I pulled in. Maybe someone just pulled in there briefly to make or

113

answer a cell phone call. Since we have no street lights up here, if you're not familiar with the road it's best to pull over and take a call."

"Guess, you're right. I was just being hyper cautious after the events at the museum. Anyway, I turned around and drove back in front of your road, saw no cars other than yours in front of the house, so I guess it's OK to go on home".

"That's very dear of you Bert! You're a good friend! It's pretty late, so go on home but know that I owe you a batch of cookies for looking out after me. Don't worry. I'm fine and as soon as I have my tea, I'll hit my bed and probably be out like a light if I follow your brandy suggestion."

"You do that, Maggie! Good night! I'll come down tomorrow and take you out for breakfast. We can strategize then and see if we can make some sense of all this. Are you calling the insurance people Monday to notify them that *Dingleton* is missing and the police are investigating the theft?"

"Yes. That's my first to do after saying my morning prayers. No sense calling, they won't be there on Sunday, but I will email my agent, who's the head of the agency in Claremont and I'm sure he'll see it and get back to me Monday."

After saying their good nights, the friends hung up. Maggie went to the cupboard and pulled out a little used bottle of brandy, stirred in some sugar and a measure of the liquid stuff and prepared to wind down with her tea and a cookie in front of the fire before turning in.

ALMA GILBERT

CHAPTER SIXTEEN

The next morning dawned with its usual preamble of birds chirping for their breakfast, cicadas beginning to tune their back legs for their morning sonatas and the occasional frog call announcing that all was well and rain could be expected later. It promised to be a hazy day that augured the possible rainstorm later. When Maggie started to slowly be aware of her early morning surroundings, all seemed so normal and pleasant.... until she remembered: Jeff was gone! He'd been brutally murdered....AND *Dingleton* was missing! The memory of the disastrous previous evening served almost like an adrenaline shot to her system: the usual aches and pains of her aging body were forgotten, the tight vise around her heart muscle seemed to be even tighter than was her expected normal this morning and the expectancy of a new day was now a grim reminder of what she needed to face.

Before starting her morning routine, Maggie quickly knelt down and said a prayer for the repose of her friend's soul. Even though Jeff was not Catholic, Maggie wanted to feel that his genuine kindness and what he had done in his life would save a very special

116

place in heaven for him. She was sure Mr. Parrish was
going to be his spirit guide and lead him to a place of
joy and peace. She also addressed the saints in heaven
and particularly St. Anthony to please keep an eye out
for *Dingleton* and bring it safely back to the museum.

She started her coffee pot going and after a quick
shower, she headed for her computer to alert the
museum's insurance agent as well as the media about
the robbery. She knew that many of the press people
kept their police scanners on and would already know
about the murder that had taken place and she could
not bring herself to write about Jeff's passing yet. It
was too close to her heart to write about it this
morning.

She was still pecking away at her computer when her
house phone rang. She saw from the caller ID that it
was the young woman reporter from one of the local
TV stations. She let the message go to her voice mail
and continued writing the e-mails she knew she must
do as the museum director. She wondered about
notifying Jeff's parents or getting their addresses. As
far as she knew they were retired and had moved to
Florida where the winters were not severe. She totally
dreaded the call she must make to them. She looked in
her computer's data base and did not find Jeff's contact
information for them in Florida. All she had was their
New Hampshire telephone number which they had
kept since they loved spending the summer and fall
months in New England.

The next call that came in was from the **Valley**

News Art Staff reporter. She did not want to talk to him either until she cleared the official museum's announcement with the board and its president, which would take place the next day when they met for their emergency meeting in the morning.

 Her cell phone rang. Thank God that only those that were close to her, like her children and selected members of the museum staff and board had that number. It was Bert asking her how she was doing and could she be ready to be taken out for a brunch somewhere near the river in Woodstock or Quechee. Gratefully she accepted and asked to go somewhere that might give them a certain amount of privacy. Her face was well known in the New Hampshire and Vermont art communities and she certainly did not want to be seen lunching out so soon after the tragedy at the museum.

 Bert suggested a quiet breakfast at a small, two hundred year old former tavern with the quaint name of Skunk Hollow Inn. After setting up a time when he could pick her up, he hung up quickly to let her finish the e-mails she must send out.

 Maggie had a number of unanswered questions in her mind she wanted to run by Bert, so the time they would spend together would be important prior to the meeting with the board.

 After finishing her e-mails, she donned comfortable flats, a sweater and a sensible but expensive tan silk skirt and hurried to the early Sunday morning Mass at

118

St. Francis of Assisi the nearest Catholic church to her other than the one in either Hanover, NH or Woodstock, VT. She knelt in her accustomed place close to the altar. The early Mass was probably the least well attended one, and this time, above all, she preferred that to a more crowded one where people who knew her well attended later in the day. She commended Jeff's soul to the angels in heaven and after lighting a candle in his name at the end of the service, she hurried home to be there when Jeff arrived to pick her up.

Bert was already waiting outside her little cottage in his sporty roadster. "Bert, could you put up the car top up, please? I don't want to go roaring up the street in an open convertible. It's not seemly under the circumstances."

Bert shook his head at her, but promptly raised the car's top and handed her a pair of dark sunglasses. "Here, you won't be recognized at the Skunk Hollow if you wear this."

"But people might think I have a hangover and need to wear them because of that!" Maggie objected eyeing the sporty sun shades doubtfully.

"More the reason that you should wear them, Maggie Winters! That will also mean they won't recognize the celebrated director of the Cornish Colony's preeminent museum. SHE would NEVER have to suffer a hangover being well known to be mostly a teetotaler who can't drink worth a darn!" he added grinning

119

mischievously at her.

Maggie could not help but grin gently at his cajoling. She knew that Bert was trying to keep her spirits up for what she knew would be a very difficult day before the board and wanted to run some early morning thoughts by him.

After they were seated at the Skunk Hollow tavern, they resumed their conversation. "Bert, you know those two sort of clear, plastic panels on either side of the museum entry door"?

"The ones by the alarm panel? Yes, I know the ones to which you are referring. Are they part of the burglar alarm system?"

"Yes. They are the ones that activate the little alarm buttons that are pasted behind each of the very valuable pieces. They are designed to trigger a special alarm if anyone going through the door is carrying a painting when the museum is open to the public and the alarm is not activated. That's in case someone had slipped by one of the volunteer docents and hidden a small work under a vest, jacket, raincoat or even a bulky purse to pass out the door undetected and unseen during regular museum visiting hours."

"Is that the same little blue button pasted on behind *Dingleton's* frame?"

"Yes."

Bert was a quick study. "Oh! That's why the frame
120

was not taken and left behind last night, so the alarm would not be activated!"

"Exactly. But what worries me is that very few people knew that *Dingleton* had that added safety feature. These people had apparently already figured that the alarm would be bypassed if the frame was left behind, right? Since the painting was not that big, and it was done on board, it could easily have been slipped under a dinner jacket or a bulky wrap and not noticed or damaged."

"How easy was it to get the painting out of the frame? Would one need extra tools or something?"

"No. Unfortunately, the pressboard that Mr. Parrish used for his paintings, was only about two tenths of an inch thick. He used four butterfly type bolts to hold it securely against the frame. All someone had to do was turn the bolts once each to release the board from the frame and the painting would be out. It was small enough and thin enough so it could easily be hidden under a coat or garment. Without the button in the frame, the alarm would not be set off!"

"Evidently, so. But who would have known that?" asked Bert.

"Other museum or gallery people who use the same thing to secure their Parrish oils from being stolen, would know that. Usually thieves just grab the painting and don't bother to discard the frame if it's small. An unusually savvy thief or else someone who's been alerted would certainly be aware of that security measure and make sure the frame got left behind so as not to activate the entry alarm."

"Who had seen the back of the painting?" Bert wanted to know.

"After Mrs. Cartwright's first offer to purchase *Dingleton* was turned down by the board, I remember she returned and stopped by the museum and talked about our security here. She asked if she could see the back of the painting on the pretext that she wanted to note what museum exhibit labels it had behind it and track where it had been shown and who had owned it. When Jeff was setting up the exhibit, it was he who took it off the wall and showed her the back of the painting. A savvy dealer like her would not have had any trouble understanding what Jeff discussed about the purpose of the little blue button attached to the frame, denoting it had the additional protection."

"Yes. But Mrs. Cartwright was found slumped outside of her car and she was not carrying *Dingleton*! When would she have had the opportunity to abscond with it? Didn't Jeff lock up the galleries when we went to sit down for supper?"

"I'm sure he did. He was very conscientious. Remember he was late coming to take his seat." added Maggie.

"Yes. But also remember that Mrs. Cartwright never did come back or sit with us after the gong was sounded announcing dinner was served. However, her assistant and the cheesy Chicago donor were sitting at table and I see them more as the type to set up the theft than Prudence!" Bert said, his brows knit in concentration.

"True. I was on the way to go looking for her in the ladies room when Denny came in to tell us that there was someone passed out in the parking area near her car. You and I rushed out and…."

"True. But everyone else stayed behind. In the confusion, someone at table could have gone to pick up *Dingleton*." was Bert's obvious thought.

"You forget, Bert. The exhibit door was locked. Jeff stayed behind to secure it and turn off the lights in the exhibit spaces as we were all headed for the dining room."

"Oh, Bert, I hope the police can come up with something and we can get our *Dingleton* back!"

The two friends had suddenly lost their appetites and pushed their plates back. Maggie guessed that there was nothing to do but wait for the police report after they had interviewed the twenty odd guests that had been in the museum….and of course, there was a board meeting next morning. Neither of them were looking forward to that! Maggie said a quick prayer and asked her guardian angel to please assign Mr. Parrish to look after her during what she knew was going to be a very unpleasant meeting the next day.

ALMA GILBERT

CHAPTER SEVENTEEN

Monday did not begin auspiciously. All the hazy skies of the day before had translated to a good size thunderstorm followed by a deluge of rain early Monday morning. The hill will be a mess, thought Maggie distractedly as she dressed in slacks, cotton shirt and low heels. No sense in wearing a silk blouse, it would only get soaked and look it, despite her umbrella and her yellow slicker. She was in first and noticed with a pang that Jeff would no longer be there ahead of her to turn off the alarm. The thought of that really kind soul being brutally slain made her angry and sad at the same time. She involuntarily gritted her teeth and vowed she would find a way to avenge his senseless death.

Denny poked his head in the front door and shouted up to her. "You O.K. this morning, Maggie? Anything I can do for you?"

Maggie appreciated his kindness. He knew how she was feeling, not having Jeff there anymore. "No, thanks, Denny. I'll be all right. Thanks for checking in on me. Will you have to do anything about the hill?"

"Nothing I CAN do, til it stops raining. But don't worry. I'm on it. Will the board be coming up later? OOPS!!! I hear your secretary's car revving up the hill, not a good thing with all that muck. She's going to get stuck and I'll have to pull her car up with my tow truck." Denny was practically out the door before he finished speaking headed for his truck and Amy Brown's car now stuck half way up the hill just as predicted.

When Amy was finally freed and had made it up the hill, she entered dripping wet and hung her mackintosh on a peg in her office next to Maggie's door. She peeked in and said. "Lots to do today, I guess, Maggie. Want me to fix you some tea and coffee before I start calling reporters back and typing out the board's agenda minutes?"

That's what Maggie liked about Amy so much. In one sentence she encapsulated all the things that have been worrying her that needed doing that morning. She'd received a couple of e-mails the night before, including one from Connie, the youngest and most enterprising of the steady museum volunteers, asking if she'd like her to be there today to help with anything. Connie wanted to know if they should get a cleaning service to clean and straighten out the room where Jeff had been killed. Maggie called Connie as soon as she arrived at work and nixed the idea of a cleaning service, remembering the yellow tape on the door.

"Jeff's work area is still sealed up, Connie. The police may need it to stay just like that. When they tell me they're finished going through the room, we'll certainly ask a cleaning service to come in. I don't want our volunteers to have to face that mess. It's too awful and painful."

She didn't need to answer the second e-mail. It was self evident from Samantha Vanderpool, requiring her attendance at the emergency board meeting. Needless to say, Maggie was not looking forward to that meeting.

Maggie heard another car negotiating the muddy hill and looked up to see who might be coming up. It was Trooper Mike Walter's police car and this time, he was driving it himself and escorting someone else from the department. Maggie went down to the closed entry door and let the men in. They were outside in the portico entrance wiping their muddy boots and shaking the moisture out of their hats.

"Maggie, this is Detective Lieutenant Lucas Lucarelli from the Vermont barracks in Montpelier. He's assigned to this murder case."

"Detective Lucarelli, I'm Maggie Winters, the museum director."

"Call me Luke, Mrs. Winters, everyone does. May I call you Maggie?"

"Yes. Please do. I'm more comfortable with that as

opposed to Mary Margaret Winters."

"Want us to take off our boots, Maggie? They're pretty muddy and I don't want to track your parquet floor with this muck!"

"You don't have to, Mike, but I'm grateful if you would."

Both men shrugged off their muddy shoes and entered the building in their stocking feet. Maggie truly appreciated their courtesy in offering to do so. The cleaning people would have a lot less to do when they came in next time. Trooper Walters led the way upstairs to what had been Jeff's workroom.

"It's best if only the police finish looking at the room, Maggie", he said donning the gloves and special paper booties for the crime scene investigation. We will probably be through with this room and your people can come in and clean up after we're done today". Saying that, the men closed the door behind them, leaving Maggie outside in the hallway.

About an hour later, the men came out and Lucarelli stuck his head in Maggie's office and said, "We removed the yellow tape, Maggie, so that you can get the room cleaned up when you want. Now can I take a look at the exhibit space from where the painting was taken?"

Maggie led them downstairs to the main exhibit room that was also sealed up with the yellow Police Crime

Scene tape. Before entering it, they had removed and discarded the soiled paper booties and donned clean ones, so any extraneous blood stains on the old ones would not be transferred elsewhere.

The room remained exactly as they had left it Saturday evening after discovering the painting missing. Before entering, Lucarelli inspected the carved entryway carefully, paying particular attention to the lock. He took out a small pocket light from the inside of his jacket, momentarily exposing his police gun's holster inside.

"Look at this, Mike", Lucarelli said to the Vermont trooper pointing at miniscule slivers by the wood holding the lock. "This was recently tampered with. It looks like a small knife was inserted here to spring the lock, and it made a few nicks on the wood while doing so."

Mike Walters nodded and took out a small pocket camera that he had evidently been using upstairs in Jeff's room. He took a couple of close-ups of the lock, nodding his assent at Lucarelli's assessment. After this was completed the men walked into the room. Nothing else had been disturbed. The only glaring discrepancy was the ludicrous empty frame hanging forlornly on the hook.

Lucarelli sat down heavily in the smooth wooden bench in the middle of the room where visitors normally sat to enjoy the different paintings and art objects all around. Facing the empty frame, he tipped his head critically and asked Maggie: "Whoever took the painting had to be in a hurry since he was evidently doing it while others were occupied either eating or going to see what had happened to that woman they found in the parking lot. Why not leave the frame on the floor after removing the art work? Why hang it back up? What does that say to you, Maggie?"

"Either he was trying to mock the staff and the visitors by hanging the empty frame where a thing of beauty had been taken, or else he was a compulsively neat nitpicker who picked up after himself."

"My thoughts exactly. The painting that was supposedly stolen: remind me again what kind of insurance value it was carrying?"

That got Maggie's goat! "SUPPOSEDLY STOLEN? Very much stolen, Detective!. It's not here anymore, is it?"

"What was its worth, Mrs. Winters, please.?" The air had just gotten a few degrees chillier.

"We queried a friend at Christie's asking what Parrish landscape oils of this size were selling for at Christie's, and she came up with the amount of $600,000."

"Isn't that an awful lot for such a little guy? Small rural museums sure must be rolling in the dough to be able to afford those numbers."

"The museum had received a generous check a week before so that we could insure it since we were not expecting to lay out any more money in insurance at this time. Our budgets are usually prepared a year in advance so that we know what we can afford to own and what we must simply borrow from other museums and private owners who many times will continue to carry their own insurance."

"Was the frame dusted for prints Saturday?" Lucarelli asked Mike Walters.

"Yep. We did not find any other prints except Maggie's here and Jeff's."

"You already have a set of their prints?"

" Yes. A few days ago, a giclee type copy that had been done while the original was being cleaned was on display and it got stolen right after it was put up. It was reported, but since it was decided that it was just a print of *Dingleton* as opposed to the original, no further inquiries were made. But we did file a burglary report just in case and had the precaution of having their prints on file since they work with highly valuable objects and we need to differentiate their prints from those of unknown others that may touch the frames or the art object itself."

"Interesting!" was Lucarelli's only comment before asking: "What the hell is a giclee?"

"A fancy and rather expensive way to prepare a copy of the original." Maggie explained that the term is French since the technology was developed there. "If

131

you didn't know what you were looking at, you'd swear it was the original."

"Interesting!" was again Lucarelli's comment.

Mike Walters drew Maggie aside and told her that the coroner had done the preliminary examination on Jeff's body. And they were still waiting for some results done on Prudence Cartwright's autopsy that had been sent to the lab in Montpelier. The contents of her stomach as well as some of the tissue from her primary organs were sent out for further testing. Evidently, the local coroner had concluded primary cause of death had been caused by a severe blow to the back of her head. It had not been discovered at first by the EMT people because Prudence had been wearing her highly coiffed wig and no blood had seeped through it to be noted until the body was taken to the morgue.

"That pushes this case into the big leagues, Maggie, and that's why Montpelier sent Lucarelli to nose around the scene of the crime," was Mike Walter's apologetic reply.

Maggie had not thought that this day could be worse than Saturday. She was fast realizing she had been wrong. She felt she needed to hold onto something to keep her balance. Mike reached across and steadied her by holding on to her arm.

"I know, Maggie. That's a lot to have hanging over this little museum: two murders and a theft of a major work, all in the same night! Our headquarters had not seen this much excitement in years, since the church building burned down Christmas Eve in '78! They put a priority to this report, otherwise it would take them about three weeks to issue their findings. Lucarelli thinks the murders are tied together, so they're going to put a rush in the pathology report. Do you want to tell your board this afternoon or do you want me to do it?"

"Thanks, Mike. I would appreciate it if you let me do it. It's my job to let them know the good as well as the bad news. If you hold off telling the papers until after five today, I would appreciate it."

"I can do that Maggie", the big Trooper said sympathetically. He knew Maggie's position as director was now probably in serious jeopardy.

As they were leaving, Lucarelli handed Maggie his card and said, "I'm going to do a little nosing around and educate myself on the prices of this type of high end art so that I can be more conversant on what we have here. Sorry if I came on too strong, Maggie. Mike Walters clued me in how long you've been here and how much this museum means to you. I'll try to help, but I must do my job the best way I know how. Here's my number. Call me any time if anything develops or you think of something I should know."

"All right, Detective. I appreciate that."

"Call me Luke", said Lucarelli. "Let's go back to being on good terms."

ALMA GILBERT

"Understood, Detective. I know you're only doing your job as I must do mine".

With that, the men walked outside, slipped into their mud covered shoes and ambled back to their car, exchanging questions and comparing notes.

Maggie walked back into the museum and walked upstairs disconsolately. She looked at her watch and seeing it was lunchtime, she decided to pass on food and have a cup of her beloved chamomile tea in her office.

At around two, Amy Brown knocked at her door and asked if she'd like something special to be prepared for the board's meeting. She had some cookies in the freezer that could be warmed up. The water, coffee and tea were staples and they had already been brought down to the boardroom. Maggie agreed readily, thanking her and busied with a report organizing her thoughts and what had been conveyed to her earlier by the Walters and Lucarelli.

Promptly at a few minutes to three, the board members led by Bert and Jim Duncan began gathering downstairs in the board room, the site where the tea had been held only a couple of days ago.

Maggie busied herself making sure everyone had copies of the minutes of the last meeting as well as pencils and pads at their disposal.

It was Jim Duncan's turn to give her an encouraging

hug and whisper gently in her ear: "COURAGE!"
Maggie looked up startled, and Jim smiled and said:
"Bert says that always encourages you when you're
facing a tough moment facing the board, so since I see
you ahead of him, I thought it would be good if you
have two voices singing the same song to you." the
amiable retired art history professor smiled knowingly
and pressed her hand warmly.

He and Maggie had worked together for years. He
had been called upon several times to write articles on
the Cornish Colony for the museum publications or
exhibits. She had reciprocated by allowing some of his
American History students long hours of her time and
help with their various thesis on American art of the
early 20th century which represented the most active
period for the many painters, sculptors and writers who
made the up bulk of the members of this prestigious
American colony. She saw Jim as a trusted friend and
was glad he had accepted their repeated invitation to
join the board of directors now that he had definitively
retired from teaching at Dartmouth.

Everyone had gathered at the time by the time three
o'clock came around except the President who was , as
usual, a fashionably late 5 or so minutes, designed to
keep the board anticipating her arrival.

She arrived in stocking feet, having tried to gun her
powerful Mercedes up the muddy hill and failed. "I
had to leave my good car for the grounds keeper to pull
out of the mud, " she began peevishly. "My shoes are
ruined. I left them outside the entrance."

Without her heels, she did not seem to tower as much which made Maggie feel a little smug to have used comfy shoes for the day, even though her psyche could have done with a little bit of heel to raise her (she thought) insignificant height of five feet to at least five feet two. Looking around and seeing everyone present and all her officers at their places, Samantha hammered the meeting open.

After the reading of the minutes, they proceeded to the reason for the meeting, namely the disastrous events of the weekend. Maggie raised her hand and said she had a report from the police that she needed to give to the board, so she was given the floor.

After finishing, Maggie looked at all the stunned faces, including Bert's. No one had expected the horrific news that Prudence Cartwright's death was now being designated as a murder, just like that of their own staff member, Jeff Andrews.

"But this is horrible! How can this museum survive the shame and the publicity of not only losing a major work that was just donated, but also having two murders occur in the premises on the same day it was installed?" Samantha groaned.

Maggie, sat down, defeated by the sense of doom everyone was feeling. She racked her brain for answers where there were none, just questions.

The silence was mercifully broken at last by Bert who spoke gently to the gathering but particularly to

Maggie. "This is more than most people have to bear in a lifetime, so it's understandable that these horrible occurrences leave us all at a loss of words. The unthinkable has happened, not in the capitals of commerce and the world, but in a gentle and simple New England town where the theft of cow or even a car seems our most egregious deed. To lose two lives and a major work of art all in the span of a couple of hours is more than the mind can take in. Given that all, we must allow those closest to the loss time to think and grieve before we start pointing fingers and asking for resignations, as we were preparing to consider, given the telephone calls prior to this meeting which most of us received from our esteemed President."

"I don't appreciate my agenda being superseded before I've had a chance to present it to the board", was Samantha's angry hiss.

"By phoning us individually today ahead of the meeting and seeking our support to dismiss our museum Director peremptorily, you HAVE presented your agenda for this meeting, Madam President," was Bert's cool reply. "But I think all the facts should be heard and consideration given to the fact that, despite your desire to hire someone younger, Mrs. Winters is the best possible choice to see this board through this difficult time given the fact that no one, NO ONE", he repeated "has her expertise and knowledge of this situation and this museum that she has."

"What you <u>don't</u> know, Bert Lincoln, is that I was called on Sunday by one of the volunteers who was pouring tea on Saturday. She asked to remain anonymous because she doesn't want to get the director into trouble, but she told me she saw her offer Mrs. Cartwright a drink of tea which may have sickened her and caused her to pass away. The museum would simply not be able to cope with the concomitant scandal if that is the case: the poisoning of a generous donor just because that donor had expressed the opinion that our director was a 'little bit too long of tooth' to continue directing this museum."

Maggie was stunned beyond responding. She had even forgotten that she had offered Prudence a cup of tea….and Prudence didn't drink it anyway, she refused it on some pretext or other, she remembered.

Three hands went up asking for the floor. Samantha yielded to Jim Duncan first since she hoped to have him suggest someone from Dartmouth to take over the museum for a little while until a suitable replacement for a director was found.

Jim stood his lean frame leaning against the board table and asked the questions that the other two hands wanted to bring up. "Casting aspersions without proof is always reprehensible but understood at difficult times like this, Madame President, but did I not just hear the report given by Maggie that the autopsy on Mrs. Cartwright gave the cause of death to having been caused by a heavy blow to the back of the head? Maggie was present with us at the dinner table when Denny discovered the body lying on the parking lot near her car. She went out with Bert and saw the body

138

for the first time. None of us knew at that time that it was there due to severe trauma to the back of the head."

Both Bert Lincoln and the board's Secretary who had also raised their hands said they were both going to make the same point.

"Madame President, " Maggie intoned solemnly. "I am perfectly willing to step down until my name is cleared."

"You're not accused of anything Maggie, other than offering Samantha a cup of tea from the same silver server that everyone else was using. Don't let anyone railroad you out of your job which you do so willingly and generously, given the salary the board gives you." volunteered Maggie's supporter Jim Duncan

Many nods of agreement followed almost unanimously up and down the board table. The vice president and the treasurer both remained silent.

"Maggie, if you don't mind, I am going to take a vote of confidence on your tenure that must remain anonymous, so I am going to ask you to step out of the room until you're called back." Samantha Vanderpool ordered, gaveling the table for good measure.

Maggie gathered her papers and without a word, stepped out of the board room and closed the door behind her. After a few minutes of further discussion Samantha called for the vote on dismissal of the current museum director with full pay for time served plus her earned retirement benefits.

It was voted down by a margin of eight Nays and only three Yeahs in favor of dismissing Maggie. Samantha accepted the loss of her pet project with a show of equanimity and asked the Treasurer to open the door and ask Maggie to return to the board room.

A few more minutes elapsed before Katherine Clark returned. "Maggie is not here. She doesn't seem to be anywhere in the museum and her car is gone. I dialed her office but do not have her cell phone to call and find out where she is. Let's give her a little time to get home and I'll call her there." Katherine let a few more minutes lapse while the board walked around, stretched and whispered to each other. She came back into the board room a few minutes later and in a voice that expressed the worry that everyone else was having, she announced: "She's not at home, either. So does any one know where she is?" No one answered.

At that point there seemed little purpose in continuing the meeting, so it was adjourned.

As everyone was departing, the only one that spoke up was Samantha. "Oh, Damn! That means I have to close up this creaky place and set the alarm on since I now seem to be the only one left around here that has the alarm code."

CHAPTER EIGHTEEN

Les Wonkrowski was also having a difficult Monday. The mysterious Chicago client, Mr. Jones, was on the phone demanding to speak to Les to find out when he could expect delivery of his promised goods. Les did not want to take this particular call after having spoken to Vito and finding out that no goods were available to be delivered at this time.

Everyone at the museum who had been interviewed pleaded absolute ignorance of what had transpired. All confirmed that Maggie Winters had come in later than all the guests other than Jeff Andrews who supposedly had been turning off the lights in the exhibit room and locking the doors securely. Jeff was the last known person who had been in the exhibit space. Les and Mr. Jones' stories as well as those of the other guests present were pretty much the same. Most everyone recalled that there had been one empty seat left at the table when the first dish was brought in and that Maggie had said she would see if Mrs. Cartwright was indisposed in the ladies room when Denny had come in through the door saying a woman was lying outside in the parking area and was not responding to his attempts to get her up.

They recalled that Mrs. Vanderpool had had everyone remain at the table until Maggie returned and it was not until the first sounds of the ambulance's siren were heard that the guests rushed to the portico to find out what was happening. Les had gone to investigate and found Prudence attempting to be resuscitated by the EMTs. He had told them that she had seemed ill when she first left the room, and he thought she would have gone to get some medication from her car's glove compartment where she usually kept an emergency supply of her blood pressure pills.

Now, in New York, Vito was as upset as Les had ever seen him. After calming him down enough to hear what he had to say on the subject of expediting the goods for the Chicago Client, he was in a dark, evil mood. As expected, both Les and Mr. Jones had been interviewed by the Vermont police about what they knew or had seen that night, and then Vito had driven the seventy or so miles to the Manchester Airport in New Hampshire so that he could catch his flight back to New York.

Now, facing his henchman, Les was coldly angry.

"What went wrong here, Vito? The first time we sent you two weeks ago, you brought back a goddam print. Now we send you again to go and pick up the original we all had seen on the wall a few minutes before while everyone's in the same room eating, and you bring back? NOTHING? Do you know what I could do to

142

you for that?"

"What original? When I broke into the room and shone my flashlight on the wall, all there was hanging there was an empty frame! If you think I'm mad, you don't know me as well as you should! I left my goddam car at the bottom of the hill so the grounds keeper who was keeping a look out for guests would not see me arriving. I climbed that fucking hill getting stuck with briars and what all…and then when I freaking break into the dark exhibit space, all I see hanging is this empty frame! Then I have to go outside where everything is going nuts and cop cars and ambulances are coming up the hill as if they were there for a convention! I had to get out of there fast and slip and slide my way down the hill to where my car was parked to get the hell out of the state and come back to Brooklyn without being spotted. To make matters worse, you said you were going to pay me and I've yet to receive bunkum! "

"You've heard the old Chinese saying, Vito: 'No tickee no laundry'. That applies here. You didn't bring back the painting, so neither Prudence or her gallery owe you shit!"

"Oh, Yeah? Neither you nor this gallery have seen the last of me!" a disgruntled Vito said, slamming the glass door to the entrance of the gallery's office which shattered, sending glass flying all around the room.

"You really should not have done that, Vito," Les hissed between closed lips, shaking his head as he would if a boy had done some naughty thing and needed to be punished, but first, Mr. Jones needed calming in Chicago.

Maggie knew that she should have stayed put and waited for the board to call her back, but her pride and her instincts were that she needed to get out and breathe. She felt herself choking back tears and she was not about to have anyone see her feeling as defeated as she did that very instant. Thank God it had stopped raining momentarily. Deftly extracting her car keys, she tossed her large canvas bag into the passenger seat, revved up the Subaru, and took the muddy hill at a much faster clip than she should have done. She fishtailed a couple of times and then the Subaru found traction and managed to get her down with a modicum of speed and a quantity of mud on its windows and carriage. She passed the turnoff to her cottage and continued uphill toward the road that forked left away from the river and climbed steadily up the side of one of the Mt. Ascutney roads. Ascutney is considered Vermont's most iconic mountain. Maggie knew that Mr. Parrish had painted it often, admiring it from his hillside home across the river in New Hampshire.

She was not aware of how long she had been driving, only that she was reaching the lookout point where many visitors enjoyed viewing the spectacular panorama of nestled towns both from New Hampshire and Vermont on either side of the Connecticut River.

It was still daylight, so no lights were yet turned on below her.

  She parked her car and walked out to the spectator's lookout point and admired the surrounding areas below the mountain. This particular spot was a place she sought often when she needed to think, to rejoice, to mourn or just to let her emotional compass come to terms with whatever was disturbing the peace of her spirit. She was not aware of how much time had lapsed when she realized that it was getting cold and her light mackintosh was not going to help her dispel the rain that would soon start again. She was after all, up in the mountain where the only light would come either from her headlights or whatever light might still be available in a given time of day. She saw the headlights of a small vehicle coming up the same road she had traveled, so she sought the comfort of her car's interior. Before she had time to insert her key and crank up the heater, the little car roared up besides hers and the familiar form of Bert Lincoln got out slamming his door for good measure.

  "I knew I'd find you here", he said opening the passenger door and slipping in the seat besides her. "I drove past your place and seeing no lights and no cars, there's only one place that you would be and sure enough, here you are!"

  Maggie was grateful for his presence, and unbidden, a couple of tears slid down her cheeks, which she embarrassedly brushed aside. "Hey!" her friend enjoined her, "Do I have that kind of charismatic charm that make ladies swoon in tears when I appear?"

"No, you don't, goof ball", Maggie said smiling at him and patting his cheek…"I was just glad to see you, is all! I guess you know me pretty well, or else that little sports car comes equipped with radar tracking. Did you ever install once of those contraptions in my Subaru that gives away my position. They're illegal for civilians to have, you know."

"I know a guy that knows about those things." was Bert's only response delivered with a knowing smile. "Anyways, I thought you'd like to know how the board voted. You're in like the proverbial Finn! Besides, when Samantha saw she was going to be on tap every single day to open and close the museum by turning the alarm off and on by herself, she had a change of heart and decided that she had been hasty and desperately wants you back. So there!" This was delivered with a wicked grin that made Maggie smile.

"How Irish are you, anyway Bert Lincoln? You can sure dish the blarney out!"

"No Irish in this pure English boy, my lady. We of the house of Orange…" he began until Maggie gave him a gentle shove and said: "Enough of the blarney. I believe you and thank you for chasing up here to tell me. Now lead me on, sweet knight, and I will follow your lights so I don't go off the mountain in one of these turns."

"I will drive sedately, My Lady. Don't want someone

of your advanced age to go off half cocked and end up down below sooner that you're expected."

"Go on, with you! I'm only six weeks older than you and don't think I haven't checked you out, Bert. You're not far behind." Somehow, her friend coming up the mountain after her had done Maggie a great deal of good and injected her with new energy to defend her position and territory. Her dander was up and she decided that staying and 'fighting the good fight' was just what was needed here. She offered a silent prayer of thanks for guardian angels of whatever ancestry and ilk or roguishness were sent.

That same evening, a New Jersey police station was notified that a body had just floated up and was bumping against one of the local beaches' pier. There was no identification found in the body, but a car that was parked near the pier was registered to a Vito Lapinski of Trenton, NJ with an expired address. No one came forth to claim the body or the car.

A long telephone conversation ensued that evening between Les and the disgruntled Chicago Client. Germaine to the interest of both parties was the fact that Les asked the client if he had sent his own messenger to "pick up the package". Mr. Jones pleaded surprise that such a question was being put up to him but after some casual banter and some not so casual exchange of words, it was admitted that Mr. Jones might have had someone looking after his interests in Vermont that may or may not have been present that evening. The bottom line was still the same, however. The 'package' had not been delivered by anyone as of that time and Mr. Jones was growing impatient with all the parties involved.

Lester informed him that as of that moment, there had been a change in management of the New York and Chicago galleries and he was now solely in charge of running those two establishments with the help of a cadre of good, solid and knowledgeable sales people that Prudence had managed to ensnare with the promise of substantial commissions at the time of sales. He promised the Chicago Client that he would get to the bottom of the painting and its disappearance.

Prudence Cartwright's funeral was postponed until the release of the body and all that the papers would say was that she was probably the victim of a sudden stroke. Lester thought that referring to a "stroke" was particularly clever on his part in the wording the staff had sent out to all the New York and Chicago papers to publish in their obituary section. It had been a stroke, all right! A "stroke of good luck" he liked to think to himself. A stroke hit the victim in the head, didn't it? Smiling to himself he busied himself with some necessary preparations for the task ahead.

He would now need to get ahead of Mr. Jones' 'Vermont connection' and solve the riddle of the painting's disappearance so he could collect the large fee that Prudence had quoted before getting hit with a 'stroke'. He smiled inwardly at his cleverness. All he must do now is try to put the pieces of the puzzle together and find out who had lifted the painting and what had been done with it. He knew one thing for sure: the million dollar tag Prudence Cartwright was going to charge Mr. Jones had just gone up to a million and a half and might even go higher depending what he had to do to find who had taken the painting and then "liberate" it.

He started by dialing different numbers up and down New York, New Jersey, Chicago and even Los Angeles. He had connections and was going to tap them all. They didn't call him the "Expediter" for nothing! He was sure that within a week, he would have a better handle of who might have purloined the Parrish.

CHAPTER NINETEEN

After following Bert's car down the winding roads of Mt. Ascutney, Maggie and he had said good night, followed by a warm hug. Bert held her a bit longer than just a friendly hug would have required and as they separated, he looked at her and said, "Remember, Maggie, that you have a lot of friends around the area and community that care deeply about you and your welfare."

Maggie did not respond, but she had not forgotten Jeff telling her of overhearing Prudence Cartwright tell Samantha that a new curator was needed because everyone had grown tired of the current director and hardly anyone other than her immediate staff and volunteers liked her anymore.

Remembering that it was because of her personal connections and old friendships that she had been able to have works donated or loaned by people such as her friend Dotty Granville of California, or the Gertrude Vanderbilt Whitney family, Prudence's hurtful and catty words became meaningless. She promised Bert she would show up as usual for her work and await to hear what the final decision of the board meant for her.

She did not have long to wait. Besides the earlier calls of Katherine Clark attempting to find her, there were three voice mails from Samantha, the last one with a long winded semi-apology if her feelings had been hurt, but that for the time being the board had decided not to take precipitous measures until the police report became available and she was to consider her job safe for the time being, of course.

Maggie was too tired to think of eating anything for supper, and after her cup of chamomile tea, she retired to bed early so that she would be as rested as possible to face the next day's happenings.

The next day dawned with what appeared to be a sincere apology from Mother Nature for her irreverent drenching of all things living the day before. The air had a feeling of freshness to it, a new promise of happy things to come if humans would only quit their complaining and let the better informed heavenly beings do their thing, The pools of water from the night before reflected the light filtering in through tree branches and formed small rainbows in unexpected nooks around the warming hills. Soon, these very same pools would be harbingers of the pesky New England mosquitoes which made their dreaded appearance every spring, helped particularly after a good drenching of the earth.

After a good's night rest and the memory of that warm

hug with which Bert had left her, Maggie's mood was definitely upbeat this morning. Maybe it was the bright light of the early day, the freshness everywhere or even perhaps her very real intuition that things would get better eventually and the museum and its personnel would return to their established routine once *Dingleton's* disappearance would be resolved... or NOT, as the case might yet turn out to be. She definitely did not want to think that might be a possibility.

She turned off the alarm at the museum as usual and walked upstairs making mental notes that she should have Denny check on the readiness of the antiquated air conditioning system, in case New England's lightning fast spring would all of a sudden turn into full fledged summer.

Maggie walked in to the exhibit room and donned a pair of white museum work gloves. As she was getting ready to lift the empty *Dingleton* frame, her expert eye caught the imperceptible tiny pencil markings on the wall which Jeff had done a few days ago prior to the installation of the new exhibit to denote the perfect placement of where the painting should be sited. Normally, after the initial installation was completed, Jeff and other staff members would make sure that there were no visible pencil marks denoting where the edge of the frame should sit.

Maggie looked at the empty frame closely. It was perfectly and exactly placed within its four designated pencil marks, as if someone had made sure it was

152

placed EXACTLY where it should be. Jeff would do that, of course, but an intruder using a flashlight in a darkened exhibit room (as it had been the night of the theft) would certainly not have seen the imperceptible little marks and placed the empty frame exactly within its assigned space....

She cocked her head quizzically and again took a closer look at the marks. Yes. They were still there and the frame exactly placed within its boundaries. She made a mental note to mention it to the detective as well as to Jim Duncan, the retired Dartmouth Art history professor who had seen his share of museum installations, including working with Jeff as one of the installation volunteers prior to many openings. It would be interesting what Jim thought about that.

Shaking her head, she decided to leave the frame just as it was until she mentioned it to Detective Lucarelli and Jim Duncan. She did not have long to wait.

At around ten a call came through her secretary announcing that Detective Lucarelli was on his way to see her from Montpelier and should be at the museum within the next thirty minutes.

After greeting him at the door where some of the early morning visitors were beginning to congregate waiting for the museum to open, Maggie checked to see that there were enough volunteers covering the three exhibit rooms and satisfying herself that his was the case, she led Lucarelli up the stairs to her office. Passing by Jeff's workroom she saw that the police yellow tapes had been removed and the room being serviced by the professional cleaning crew who had been called in. As they passed it, she made a quick sign of the cross and a hurried prayer for the repose of his spirit.

Lucarelli who did not miss much, nodded his understanding of her gesture. "He's in a better place, Maggie", he said sympathetically. "Were you two close?"

"I was very fond of him, Lieutenant and he was my second in command here at the museum. Jeff was a fuss budget and very picky about his work, but I guess conservators are artists at heart, and they have a responsibility for the works entrusted to their care".

"Please call me Luke," he reminded her, as they sat down in her office. "Let's talk about the post mortems on the two bodies. The cut to Jeff's throat was incisive and quick. It appears that his assailant grabbed him from behind by the hair, bent his head back and made the cut. The pathologist feels that the stiletto type dagger was held in the assailant's left hand because it goes from right to left, so we will be looking at our data bases for left handed individuals that might fit the profile."

"And what's the profile, Lieutenant…. I mean Luke?"

"It's too early for us to have a complete profile, but we have some thoughts that besides being a lefty, the assailant was taller than his victim and probably stronger. That can be deduced by the victim's wound in the neck. The assailant was probably a head taller than the victim."

"Jeff was not very tall, Luke. He was willowy and probably five feet seven or eight. I know because we were always being teased about hanging paintings a little too low for the common person's height. Although he towered over me, that's because I'm only five feet two in heels."

"My men found some mud tracings in the front portico as if someone had trekked up the hill and discarded his boots before entering in his stocking feet probably so as to minimize noise and leave no footprints inside. That would have to have taken place when everyone was in the dining room. As if he knew that he would have a small window of time to come in, jimmy the lock, remove the painting and then leave while people were in the dining room. Then, if we're talking about the same guy that removed the painting and killed Jeff, what happened to the painting while he was busy being an assassin? He needed to have both hands free to do the deed. We may be talking about two different people here."

"TWO people??" was Maggie's frightened exclamation.

"Yes. I'm leaning to two different individuals. One who broke in stealthily leaving his muddy boots outside, came in, jimmied the door, removed the painting from the frame, slipped it under his clothing and left the way he came while people were just finishing their first course. Then, a second guy comes in during the time everyone's distracted with the Cartwright body in the parking area and milling around outside."

"Let's say your guy Jeff gets nervous about security, goes to check if the exhibit room is locked like he left it, finds it open and hightails it for his work area to go call the police and sound the alarm. What if the second guy shows up, finds the painting missing, decides to leave by a different door not blocked by the lookers waiting to find out what happened to the dame in the parking lot, sees this guy going upstairs follows him, finds him getting ready to call the cops and finishes him since he's had a good look at him and probably thinks this might be the one who took the painting."

"The guy pulls out his stiletto and finishes him nice and quiet and then is free to exit via the servant's entrance or the fire escape in the back of the house. Then slow and easy, he mingles with the lookers and makes his way out the way he came, no blood spatters or nothing because he did the deed from the back of the victim. We're still hoping to find a murder weapon which surely must have been discarded if the murderer was going to mingle with the people outside. No sense in mucking around with a bloody knife somewhere in your possession."

"You understand these are just conjectures at this point. We need a break or a little evidence upon which to hang our crime solving hats. Oh, and Maggie, we

156

were able to lift one print near where the muddy boots
would have been. Almost as if the owner of the boots
had momentarily steadied himself low down in the wall
while he slipped out of his boots. Evidently, he had not
yet seen the need to slip on rubber gloves until after he
entered the premises. We're running it through our
data bases and have not had a hit, so we gave it to the
FBI who's running it through their national data files."

"Well, that's certainly good news, Luke. Maybe the
FBI will have a name for you that might lead us to
whoever lifted the painting."

"Yeah, maybe, Maggie. Now do you want to hear the
not so good news?"

Maggie was startled. What else could be coming up
now? She felt her stomach knotting up in the familiar
way when there was a need for either the 'flee or fight'
syndrome.

"Remember that I told you that when the pathologist
first examined the body of Mrs. Cartwright, he found
an indentation in the back of her cranium that had left
a little bleeding which had not been noticed right away
since she was wearing a wig. We knew that to be the
cause of death and is so listed in the death certificate he
signed. However, when the contents of her stomach
were examined, there was evidence of that being the
reason that caused her initially to feel ill and stagger
outside to her car in search of some prescription
medicine she kept in the glove compartment. The
stomach contents denote a toxic substance that was not

157

enough to kill her, but enough to make her ill. It looks as if somebody may have attempted to kill her by administering a lethal poison into her system. There were only trace amounts of it, as if she had only tasted something and left the rest without taking a full helping. Was she drinking wine or something else that might have contained the poison? This had to happen before dinner because her stomach contents did not contain any amount of food. We're still waiting to have the toxicology report to see what kind of poison was administered. That should come in about a week or more. It usually takes a little more time, although we did ask for it to be examined ASAP."

 Maggie was stunned! No wonder Samantha Vanderpool was so distraught when she was told by one of the older volunteers that Maggie had been seen pouring Prudence a cup of tea. "

 "But everyone was drinking the same tea!!!", she thought. The only carafe that was ALWAYS set aside for individual use was the one Jeff prepared for himself whenever a formal tea was set up. It was regularly made up by him of a special mixture of flowers and tea leaves that he drank daily instead of coffee. He even made and kept a jar of the special honey that he used. It was kept separately for him in the museum's staff room and marked: "JEFF'S HONEY".

 Lucarelli went on minutely describing what had led the pathologist to request a toxicology exam on the stomach's contents.

"The reason we're concerned, Maggie, is that since there were no appreciable food contents in the deceased body, it had to be whatever she had ingested in liquid form that had caused imperceptible bleeding of the stomach and adjacent tissues. She would have immediately felt ill with the effects that would have caused sweating and blood pressure to drop sharply, but whatever she ingested would not have been enough to kill her, just make her feel nauseous and unwell and probably given her a heck of a stomach ache. What we do know is that she ingested something at that tea party which gave her that kind of immediate reaction."

"I'm grateful for the information, Luke, but I don't know what to tell you. I gave her a cup of the same tea I, and most of the other guests who were not drinking cocktails, were having. I remember putting my own cup down on the table so I could pick up the carafe and pour her a cup."

"Just giving you a head's up, Maggie. I have real good crime instincts, and I don't think you would be one of our likely suspects to do away with anyone in the vicinity. I've read up on you, of course, and know you've been a constant supporter and rooter for this little museum for nearly thirty years. Just don't see you doing away with the competition or even an annoying type of person as the deceased seemed to have been according to some of the people I interviewed, that's all. Much as you might have reason to dislike her," he added knowingly.

"Keep in touch, Maggie. Just don't plan to leave town

to go see your friends in California, yet."

"I won't be going anywhere, Luke. Thanks for the heads up. I truly appreciate it!"

When Detective Lucarelli left, Maggie made a quick phone calls to contact Bert and Jim Duncan asking if they could drop by the museum sometime after lunch for a quick consultation. Both men said they'd be free after three and would drop by to talk to her then. The lunch hour and afternoon seemed to drag for Maggie until the men were announced and brought into her office.

"I feel I need to be outside guys. Do you mind if we sit by the little table near the big oak? I also need to get your take on something I just noticed and I want to fill you in on what Detective Lucarelli just told me this morning." The men agreed and the three friends trooped downstairs and looked in on the exhibit area. The little empty frame was still cordoned off with yellow police tape and seemed to be a big point of interest to all who came in. The local newspapers: **Valley News, Keene Sentinel**, **Burlington Free Press** and even the **Boston Globe** and the **New York Times** had all run stories on the disappearance and likely theft of the Parrish oil. The story had tripled the museum attendance and people were milling around the site where *Dingleton* had once hung alongside the other major pieces.

On the way, Maggie silently pointed surreptitiously at the barely visible pencil marks indicating where

Dingleton should be hung and without saying a word in front of the visitors and curious onlookers, she led both board members outside to sit under the old oak.

"Were those marks always on the wall here, Maggie? I had not noticed them before or on the other paintings, for that matter", was Jim's first query.

"Can't say that I noticed them either", was Bert's corroborating response. Both of the men had volunteered from time to time to help the small museum staff hang the exhibits. The thin pencil marks were always there, but then meticulously erased by Jeff who was the chief installer when the paintings had all been placed in their assigned spots.

"The only thing that I can come up with", said Maggie speaking slowly and trying hard to remember, "was that the frame without the painting had been placed there by Jeff before the exhibit opened since *Dingleton* was upstairs still drying after it had been cleaned and varnished. Maybe Jeff left the marks so that he would place it exactly in the spot later after the painting was put back into its frame the morning of the opening, forgetting his usual habit of erasing the pencil marks on the wall once the painting was hung. We were all in a terrific rush, as usual just before an opening. Jeff had brought his suit here so he would not have to rush home to change and urged that I take a couple of hours off before the opening to rest and change into formal attire."

"Yeah, that's true, but I don't see whoever took it to

take the time to meticulously place the frame off the floor back on its precise spot. Remember, it was someone working in the dark and with the pressure that he not be discovered."

"It doesn't make sense, does it?" was Bert's meditative reply. "No one would be that much of a nit picker like Jeff was in order to make sure an empty frame was in exactly the right spot."

"Hmm", was Maggie's meditative reply.

"Quiet: Woman Mulling!" was Bert's impudent retort. "Run by us what you're thinking, Maggie, after all, you called us in to consult with you!" he grinned roguishly.

"What IF, just bear with me for a moment: what if Jeff himself took the painting down before joining us and put it away somewhere."

"But that's silly, Maggie! The exhibit had just been put up for the lenders and donors before the public saw it. Why would Jeff take the painting down and if he DID take it down, where would he have placed it? Makes no sense to me... and if he DID take it down when would he have done it or where would have put it?" was Jim's puzzled comment.

"THE VAULT! Did anyone look for it in the vault upstairs? It's the adjacent room to your office and Jeff's work place!" was Bert's excited thought. Without a word, the three friends rushed upstairs in a most unseemly hurry within a museum's premises.

"Only three of us have the combination: Samantha, Jeff and I" was Maggie's breathless announcement when they reached the upstairs. They hurried into the room where the massive vault had been sited nearly a hundred years before. Maggie knew the combination by memory but in her excitement, she misplaced one of the numbers and had to start two or three times before the venerable vault would click its welcome and deign to open its door for the anxious spectators. Nothing seemed out of place or disturbed. The empty boxes where other art works had been sent by lenders to the museum lay orderly and sealed like soldiers waiting in parade rest. No precious *Dingleton* in sight or on any of the empty storage shelves arranged in the periphery of the vault where the museum's owned art was stored when it was not on display downstairs.

The adrenaline expended with the rush upstairs in the hope of finding the little painting on board had left the three friends feeling infinitely more tired when it was evident that the little oil Parrish had named *Dingleton* was nowhere in site on any of the shelves.

"OH! I had so hoped it might be here, safe and secure," was Maggie's saddened comment.

"We know how you feel Maggie, and we're not nearly as invested in its recovery as you evidently must be! Let's put our thinking caps on and see if we can come up with something, anything else!" was Bert's sympathetic suggestion.

The three friends proceeded downstairs not nearly as hurriedly or excitedly as they had gone up, and found a seat again under the lovely spreading oak. After several suggestions and questions, Jim asked Bert: "Who was that Vermont mystery detective writer that spoke here last year during the annual fund raising event?"

"Archer Mayor" answered Maggie and Bert simultaneously, and saying it, they both smiled at each other for thinking the same thing and answering it jointly.

"He was very kind to the museum and donated a number of his detective books. Evidently, he is a former death investigator for the Vermont State Medical Examiner's office, had been a volunteer EMT for a long time and also worked in the Windham County Sheriff's department for a while, so he's very savvy in these matters. Maybe I could ring him up and ask if he could drive down from his home in Newfane and have lunch with us and maybe have his brain picked on while he's at it!"

"Maggie Winters, that's one of the best ideas you've had in a long time. Go for it!" was their enthusiastic reply.

"Just remember: No flirting! He's younger than us!" Bert added giving her a wink and a broad smile.

CHAPTER TWENTY

There was an urgent call from Mr. Jones waiting for Lester when he arrived at the New York gallery the following morning. He was not in a sparkling mood and the traffic and the congestion in the streets had done nothing to lighten his outlook.

"Tell the receptionist I'm not to be disturbed" was the curt command when he came in and went directly to the office Prudence Cartwright had once occupied. His feet planted squarely on the good mahogany desk, he drew out his cell phone and dialed a number that had been left for an office in Chicago's disreputable North Government Pier.

"Shipping" was the brusque greeting.

Les gave them the name under which Mr. Jones was doing business and was connected to the boss-man as he was referred to in his office.

"When am I getting the goods I ordered from Vermont?" was the curt opening. "By the way, I didn't enjoy having the cops give me the once over at the party, Lester. The less I'm known the better I like it. It's not good for my business to have encounters of the kind you put me through in that dinky town in Vermont. I don't like cops and they don't like me. At least that high society dame that's president of the board bragged about me being a big donor so they didn't give me too much of a bad time. By the way, I'm losing patience with you and I'm not known as a patient man. When do I get the delivery I am paying for?"

"That's why I'm calling. I'm taking over the business and will see to it myself that the object gets picked up if I have to do it myself. I'm getting mighty annoyed by the director there. I think she knows more than is good for her. Her flunky overheard you talking to me just before we went out to the dining room. I know he heard you asking me if I had made arrangements to secure the little work. I bet that had something to do with my guy not finding the painting when he broke in and jimmied the lock to the exhibit room. Some smart aleck must have taken it out of the frame and hidden it."

I followed him upstairs and heard his dialing the local cops, so I had to take care of him before he spilled the beans. Don't worry. I wore gloves and no one is the wiser."

"You imbecile! I don't want any of this shit to reflect on our dealings."

"I told you I was taking care of it. The flunky never

even got a chance to say who was calling or what his business was. I looked around his work room and didn't see the painting, so I'm going to put in an appearance myself and see what I find out. They're treating it as a robbery, but all of us saw the painting in the exhibit just a few minutes before, so it has to be around. Maybe the goody-goody director wants to keep it for herself and has it stashed somewhere and is playing dumb for the cops."

"You're not sending the goon you sent there twice before are you?"

There was a moment's pause and then Les said. "Unfortunately, he met with an accident recently. Just read the cops fished a body out of the water near the piers who has yet to be identified, and I just bet something like that happened to Vito."

"Just make sure you don't leave any traces of your dealings with him. You sure that was Vito they fished out?"

"Positive. The Vermont police sent a copy of the coroner's report to the gallery here. They list the cause of death as a forceful blow to the back of the head. One of the few things found in the glove compartment of his abandoned car at the dock was his usual weapon of choice: the cudgel. The dumb ass had even carved his initials on the wood handle."

"Why would he off Prudence?"

"Reckon he'd been pissed off at her. She didn't pay him the first time when he brought her a stupid print instead of the original, called him all kinds of names which must have irked him a little, I guess. And say he goes, all nice and easy again, breaks into the locked room and what does he find this time? An empty frame on the wall, that's what. He must have been itching to get his hands on her thinking she was setting him up, and sees her stumbling towards her car. Vito was not known for thinking things over beforehand. Probably sneaked in behind her and that was the end of his frustration!"

"So when you figured that out, you took care of Vito, and sent him to pay a visit to the fishes, did you? How did you get him to meet you at the dock?"

"Told him a little white fib that I was going to settle accounts for what Prudence didn't pay him and for him to get out of town quick. He took the bait and that was the end of Vito Lipinski.

"You do good work, Les!"

"They call me the Expediter, don't they?" Was the smirking reply over the line. "I'll take care of our business in Vermont personally. If necessary, I'll put a bullet between her eyes if the little old lady doesn't come up with where she hid the goods."

"I suggest you take care of business soonest, Les, and get rid of her anyway. We don't want her to sing sad songs to the police about you."

Before Maggie headed home, Amy, her secretary stuck her head through the door and said, "You might want to take this call, Maggie. It's Detective Lucarelli."

"We've had a bit of good news, Maggie. Evidently the single print my men found in the portico by where the intruder had left his shoes just had a hit in the FBI files. They matched it to a low life type whom they fished out of the water at the New Jersey pier. Bit player for the big guys, an enforcer they used to clean up some of their less attractive unfinished jobs. It appears a non-registered car he was using had a cosh under the driver's seat."

"A what, Luke?"

"Probably not a word you're used to in the museum, Maggie. A cosh is a so-called blackjack these types use to bash people's brains in. He had conveniently carved his initials: 'V.L' on the wood handle, so that with the print we found and sent the FBI made their search a whole lot easier. Interesting that whoever cleaned out his car and stripped it of identification did not find the cosh under the seat. He must have tossed it there after that single blow to Mrs. Cartwright's head. They're sending it to Montpelier to our pathologist who's going to match the blow in the cranium to the outline of the cosh, and if it does, we know pretty well who was her killer."

"That is so good to know, Luke. I'm grateful you

shared that piece of information with me. You don't know the nightmares I've been having."

"You're a good person Maggie. Most everyone in town sings your praises....with one or two exceptions which shall be nameless, but I guess you know who they may be. This is still pretty hush-hush, so please don't spread it around. "

"I won't Luke....Oh, wait: May I share it with Bert Lincoln, one of my most supportive board members?"

"Yeah, I guess you can. Rumor says you're pretty sweet on the guy."

"No, I'm not!" was the emphatic denial..."Not saying however that I've noticed that HE is as you say 'sweet' on ME." With that said, Maggie smiled gratefully at the phone before hanging it and immediately dialed Bert to give him the glad news.

One of the first questions Bert asked her was to see if he had gotten hold of Archer Mayor. "He must be on a book tour, Bert. But I'll keep trying." And then Maggie happily told him about the call from Lucarelli...(skipping any mention of his comments about 'her being sweet' on him, of course).

"Things are looking up, Maggie! Just heard from Samantha notifying the board members that Prudence's associate...what's his name?"

"Lester."

"Yeah, Lester. He's going to come in later to collect Mrs. Cartwright's ashes as soon as the pathology department releases it to the mortuary in Windsor. Guess for a reason unbeknown to most of us, he wants to stop by the museum and see if there are any more news on finding the little painting."

"FINDING THE PAINTING?" Maggie almost went ballistic. "We did not 'misplace it' Bert. It was stolen!"

"Whoa, easy there...keep your knickers on!" was Bert's impudent comment. "I was just saying what I was told."

"You're right, Bert! I have no call to be jumping on you."

"Lady, you may jump my bones ANYTIME the thought occurs to you. OOPSIE!!! better hang up before I get into more hot water." With a smile in his voice, Bert hung up leaving Maggie pondering what he had just said in light of what Lucarelli had mentioned earlier about her feelings for Bert...OR his feelings for HER, she amended quickly to herself.

The next morning dawned with a perfect Vermont depiction of the rare beauty that Mother Nature could, when she felt like it, impart on lowly mortals below. The sunlight came in pouring over the flower boxes in the window and wood thrushes gushed their enjoyment for the beauty of the day to lure their lady loves to adventuresome flights of fancy with them. A mild seventy-degree temperature augured a warming trend that summer might not be that far in the future. Maggie threw her windows open and enjoyed the breeze that fluttered the sheers that she installed each spring and summer once the numbing cold of winter and early spring had safely departed to visit cooler climes in Canada.

For the first time since *Dingleton* had been taken, she felt hopeful, that somehow, she'd see it again. Maybe it was the late spring day with summer just around the corner that invited such optimism.

However, Maggie's happy reveries were interrupted by a furious ringing of her phone. "Who in heavens would be calling me at 7:15?" she said looking at the clock on her coffee maker where she was preparing her daily two cups of decaffeinated. She shouldn't have asked. The imperious tones of Samantha Vanderpool were a jarring note on her happy earlier reflections.

"Margaret, I just received a call from Mrs. Cartwright's associate, Les...Les..."

"Wonkrowski." Maggie ventured helpfully.

"God! I hate those foreign names! Yes. Les whatever. His office was just notified yesterday that her unfortunate demise on our museum grounds was caused by a severe blow to the back of her head."

"Yes. I had heard that too from Detective Lucarelli yesterday".

"The very real problem, dear, that the museum is
172

facing, is that the preliminary toxicology report on the contents of her mostly empty stomach contained a small amount of a very toxic poison that was probably ingested during our tea. The publicity will kill this small museum. We can't afford to have that being released to the papers!"

"Oh, dear God! Just when I was beginning to feel hopeful that this would eventually be resolved by the police. And now this!" Maggie involuntarily slumped on her small two-seater couch in the cottage's neat but tiny living room, left wondering how Samantha had heard of this already.

"I think that the reason for the sudden proposed visit by Les....whatever his name is... must be related to that. I hope he does not plan to sue the museum on behalf of the bereaved family. They said they were faxing your office with the official report on the toxicology found. If you will meet me at the museum by 8:00 a.m. we can go ahead and see what it says so that I can inform the board for their suggestions on how to proceed. As I'm sure you MUST realize, this impacts greatly on you since you were seen by one of the volunteers as offering her a cup of tea."

"But Prudence, it was the same tea I, you and all the other people were drinking." Maggie started to say not realizing that the president of the board had ended the conversation abruptly and was no longer on line.

"Oh, dear God! Please help me!" were the only words the harried director could manage....and then, to

173

herself: "I'm sure calling on You, Lord, a lot lately!" She pulled the plug on the coffee brewer and was out her cottage door within ten minutes after receiving the startling call from the president of the board. She revved her Subaru up the now mostly dry hill, pulled into the parking lot with the "Museum Staff Parking" designation and hurried to open the door and turn off the red blinking light of the alarm, hurrying upstairs.

She threw her purse on the floor behind her desk and hurried to see what the FAX machine had received. She was not disappointed. Not only one FAX from the Cartwright Gallery in New York, there was also the official police and toxicology report that Detective Lucarelli had said he'd send as soon as he received it. They had both been sent the evening before long after museum hours.

CHAPTER TWENTY ONE

Both Faxes were about essentially the same matter. The official one from the Coroner's Office in Montpelier containing the cause of death as listed by a severe blow to the back of the head with a blunt instrument probably a blackjack, and the STAT Toxicology report from the pathologist in Montpelier as received from their Toxicology Department.

Maggie quickly scrolled the fax pages to the Toxicology report which stated:

Although this Department thoroughly agrees with the pathology report that death was caused by a blow to the back of the head, it is of interest that the contents of the stomach, although few were very specific: an extremely poisonous substance was found in the deceased's organs, ingested probably near the time of death because the contents remained in the stomach and immediate bladder area. The small quantity that was still in the body was certainly not enough to cause death, but it

175

would have given the deceased some very
uncomfortable moments within an hour or two
after ingestion that would have included:

Nausea, physical irritation, drooling,
vomiting, increased tear formation,
perspiration, slowing of pulse, lowering
of blood pressure, diarrhea, seizure
and with a normal amount would have
been followed by coma and death.

Since the quantity of the toxic
substance was very small, it would not
have resulted in death.

SCIENTIFIC NAME: *Rhododendrom
ponticum, R. arborescens
rhododendrum (azalea)*

TOXICITY: Maximum (6)

DEADLY PARTS: All

REACTION TIME: For a complete
dosage, no longer than six hours,
however, given the fact that only a very
small amount was found, this would not
have caused death for the victim.

NOTES: Evergreen shrubs have bell
shaped, showy flowers, but no odor
and grow in Canada, New England to
the Appalachians, and on the Pacific

Coast of the United States. Azalea flowers, another variety, are funnel shaped, often fragrant. The Greeks found that honey from the bees that fed on azaleas, rhododendrums, oleander or dwarf laurel was poisonous. Drinking tea flavored with this honey from these plants with miniscule amount of the deadly poison may be used by arthritic persons over a period of time without any of the adverse results noted above. [3]

Signed:

The report was signed and dated the day before by the resident Toxicologist in Montpelier.

Maggie sat down heavily on her office chair and looked again at the report.
"Azaleas? Rhododendrum?" Both of the flowers were in bloom near the entrance of the museum. Stunned, she remained immobile at her desk until she heard Samantha opening the front door with her key, pausing briefly to note that the alarm was set Green denoting it was turned off, and then calling out before going up the

---

[3] <u>Book of Poisons</u>. Stevens, Serita. 2007. Writer's Digest Books, Cincinnati, OH. pp. 64-65

stairs.

"Margaret? Margaret? Are you upstairs in your office?" When she heard a weak reply she ascended and marched into the director's room with fire in her eyes.

"May I review the faxes the museum was sent?" was her only comment upon entering the director's office.

Without a word, Maggie pushed the faxes over to the front of her desk. Samantha sat down heavily on the visitor's chair and proceeded to read them through.

Samantha finished reading and dropped the papers down on the director's desk. There were a few minutes of uncomfortable silence between the two women. Then the President spoke first.

"It seems clear from the report that the cause of death was the fracture of her skull and not from anything she had ingested that you may, or may not, have given her. If the museum can prove that the cup you poured was from the main carafes that everyone else was using, your culpability in her death may not be able to be proven. I will speak again to the volunteer that saw you give her a cup and see if she can attest it was from the same tea everyone else was being served. I will call her as soon as I get outside and use my cell phone from the car. In the meantime, I believe the museum should be closed tomorrow during the time of Jeff Andrews' funeral. I have ordered suitable flowers and would appreciate representation at the service from all the museum staff and as many of our volunteers that care to attend."

She took a breath and seemed to gather her thoughts together. "In the meantime, I have a very trying day ahead of me. Mrs. Cartwright's associate, (Samantha still had problems remembering his name) will be in later today to talk to us about any culpability the museum and its board may or may not have in this matter. I have taken the precaution of asking the museum's attorney to attend the meeting and hopefully join us for a more convivial lunch at Ron Santini's restaurant".

With this, Samantha swept from the office without as much as a good-bye word. Going down the staircase, she almost collided with Amy Brown who was coming in to work.

"Anything you want me to concentrate on today, boss?" she said, sticking her head in Maggie's office.

Maggie nodded distractedly and asked her to notify all the staff and volunteers about Jeff's funeral the next morning. "Is Connie scheduled in today for volunteer duty? Please ask her to come into my office when she does."

Amy nodded and added: "Let me bring you some of your chamomile tea and you look as if you need a hug."

Am I that transparent?, Maggie thought ruefully, but

said, "Hugs are always welcome here!" She gratefully received the proffered hug then sat down and began shuffling the papers on her desk. "And, Amy, please call Bert Lincoln and ask him if he has a little time today to view some papers with me."

"Will do, Maggie," her secretary said and going out almost collided with the tall hefty figure of Denny Grant coming up the steps.

"Boss in, Amy? Got something to show her."

"Sure, Denny. She's always in for you! "

"Hi, Maggie. Got something here for you. May I close the door?"

"Of course, Denny. What do you have with you?" Maggie asked looking curiously at the wrapped newspapers parcel which Denny had with him.

"Now, don't be startled, dear." said the grounds keeper, who had known Maggie for over forty years, lapsing unwittingly into using a term of endearment he only very occasionally used and never in the ears of the public. They were both of the same age and had worked in the museum for approximately the same number of years. He liked to say he always had her back and Maggie's usual retort was: "And I have yours!"

"My boys and I were clearing some of the overgrown acreage next to the parking lot and look what we found there." Denny carefully unwrapped the newspapers to
180

reveal a very wicked looking stiletto knife with a blade that appeared covered with rusty stains and remnants of wet leaves clinging to it. He looked at Maggie to gage her reaction and saw the immediate horror in her eyes at the recognition that perhaps they were looking at the murder weapon that had killed Jeff Andrews.

After a minute of shocked silence, Maggie gathered her wits and said: "Cover that thing up, Denny. I'm going to call Detective Lucarelli right now". She fumbled around with trembling hands in her purse, located Luke's card with his cell number and punched it into her phone.

"Lucarelli." The detective's gruff voice came on the line. Evidently seeing the museum's number on his screen, he added a little more cordially, "What's up, Maggie?"

The museum director in a quivery voice told him what Denny had just found while clearing the acreage next to the parking lot. "Don't touch it, Maggie. I want to see if there are any preserved prints on it. Ask your grounds keeper if he touched any part of it." Maggie obliged and asked Denny while he still stood there behind her desk.

"Did you touch it Denny?"

"Didn't touch it. Was wearing working gloves. Put it on the floor of the tractor and then covered it with these newspapers to bring it in here."

Evidently, the detective could hear Denny's answer. Lucarelli's comment was brief. "Good. I'll be there within the hour. Keep the knife out of sight but in a safe place, Maggie." The line went dead after that.

"Denny, will you be around if Detective Lucarelli needs to talk to you?

"Sure, Maggie. Brought my lunch today because I plan to clean out the hive on that Azalea tree by the museum. Volunteers have been complaining that bees are coming into the museum and want me to get rid of the hive. Now that Jeff is gone, he won't miss the honey combs I used to bring in to him to get the honey for his tea."

Maggie was struck momentarily dumb for the next few seconds.

"Did I say something wrong, Maggie?" Denny's concerned face mirrored his caring for the elderly director.

"No, Denny. You didn't. Sit down for a moment or two while I think something through." Without waiting for an answer from her grounds keeper, Maggie went to the filing cabinet where she had placed the faxed reports from the toxicology expert.

She scanned quickly over the main parts and came to the final Notes which the toxicologist had added at the end of the report:

The Greeks found that honey from the bees that fed on azaleas, rhododendrums, oleander or dwarf laurel was poisonous. Drinking tea flavored with this honey from these plants with miniscule amount of the deadly poison may be used by arthritic persons over a period of time without any of the adverse results noted above.

She hurriedly took the FAX and copied the Notes to share with Lucarelli and Bert if he came in. Then, re-entering her office she approached Denny still sitting patiently waiting for her and said putting her hand gratefully on his shoulder, "Denny, you have been an immense help to me today. May God love you and repay what you have done for us here at the museum. When I can, I will tell you how much of a big help you've been once I have clarified this with a couple of people. In the meantime, I would be very grateful if, before you dispose of the beehive, that you bring me a honeycomb such as you used to give Jeff so I can pass it to Detective Lucarelli."

"Sure thing, Maggie, I'll go do it right now and wrap the hive itself in some aluminum foil wrap I have in the tool room." With that, Denny left the office and Maggie could hear his work boots clumping down the stairs and out the front door.

"Amy, were you able to get Bert Lincoln on the phone?"

"Yes, I was, Maggie. Didn't want to interrupt while Denny was in your office. Bert said he'd be here within twenty minutes as soon as he showered cause he'd been working outside and needed a little deodorizing before he came in the museum," she said grinning. "By the way, I have now contacted all the staff about Jeff's funeral tomorrow and everyone will be there. Do you still need to see Connie? She's here at the museum now. I told her you had someone in the office but I would let her know when you were available to see her."

"Thanks, Amy. I'm ready now if she's available. Were you also able to contact our list of volunteers about Jeff's funeral?"

"I'm still working on it, Maggie. Some were not home when I called, so I left messages for them."

Within minutes, a soft tap at her door let Maggie know that Connie was there. "Come in, Connie. Thanks for coming up."

"No problem, Maggie. Do you have a specific job you'd like for me to concentrate on today?"

"Yes, I do, Connie. You know that Jeff's funeral is tomorrow. The girl nodded her assent silently. "Yes. I plan to be there".

"Jeff had some of his personal belongings not only his work room, like some of the pictures he'd taken of the landscapes in the area, but also photos of his mom and dad that I've gathered in a box to take his parents tomorrow. I need to have you do me a special favor: go to the staff lunchroom where Jeff kept his own tea mug, his copper tea carafe, personal teas he concocted himself and a jar of honey he made from the honey combs Denny gave him from our beehive outside the museum."

"Yes. That funny tea mug he had was a gift from one of the Vermont Public Radio fundraisers."

"Yes. I know it well. I teased him often about it because he always had the public station playing classical music in his workroom. I am particularly interested in his copper tea carafe and the honey he used. If you would be kind enough to collect them for me and bring them in a box to my office now, I would appreciate it."

"Will do, Maggie. Be right back." Saying that, the young volunteer left her office and practically collided with Bert Lincoln who was just about to knock on the door.

"Whoa, young lady, you practically caused this old man to flip over down the stairs", he teased her genially. Seeing the director, he smiled at her genially, and said. "Heard my presence was required here on the double. What's cooking, Maggie?"

Maggie briefed him on the reports that had come in from toxicology that morning and showed him a copy of the fax she had made on the notes about the honey which the toxicologist had added.

"Had no idea that was relevant, but evidently you seem to think it is, young lady, so tell me what's so dang important about this."

"The part about the <u>honey</u>, Bert. Jeff used the honeycombs from outside in our Azalea bush that Denny provided him with each month or so…could the honey that was used to flavor the tea I served him have been from the azalea bush outside?"

"If I remember correctly, Maggie, honey was not being offered with the teas because it can be messy. Sugar and sugar substitutes were the sweetening being offered."

Thinking back, Maggie's memory was the same. She felt crestfallen and was just about to sit back at her desk when a polite knock at the door with Connie carrying Jeff's tea things in a box announced her presence.

"Sorry to disturb you, Maggie, but here's what you asked me to get. The copper carafe was a little too tall, so I had to lay it down in the box along with the teas, honey and his VPR mug. Whenever we served teas to board members, donors or lenders, Jeff would always insist on having his own ugly copper carafe some place where he could get at it and it would not be obvious. The honey was a little sticky so I wiped it well with a wet cloth so it wouldn't get over everything. I know that when Jeff offered Mrs. Cartwright some of his own tea with his special honey, he had to wipe down the honey jar, too."

Maggie was stunned momentarily. Jeff had offered Prudence some of his tea?

"Wait a minute, dear. Did you say Jeff offered Mrs. Cartwright some of his own tea? Why was that?"

"That's what I saw when I was picking up the tea cups that people had left on the tea table. You remember you had poured Mrs. Cartwright a cup of tea? Just after you turned away, she took a sip, and made a face saying to no one in particular: 'This tasteless tea was probably made with tea bags instead of properly steamed in a teapot'. Jeff was standing by her when she said that and that's when he offered her some of his own tea that he brewed with natural plants and herbs and flavored with local honey. He poured her a brand new cup from his copper carafe. She took a teaspoon of his honey and sipped it briefly until he turned away and then left it as she did your cup right on the serving table. I thought that was not being mannerly, but of course, I could not say anything so I picked up that cup too, and took it to the kitchen for washing."

Bert and Maggie immediately exchanged glances and wordlessly conveyed to each other the importance of what Connie had just shared.

"Connie, dear. You have no idea what importance that has for me. Will you be around a bit longer? I'd like you to relate that to Detective Lucarelli who should be coming within the next half hour. It will help him immensely with his investigation."

"Sure, Maggie. Glad to be of help! I'm on duty at the museum until three p.m. today."

As soon as the door closed, Bert came around Maggie's desk and gave her a huge bear hug, lifting her literally off the floor and causing the director some unexpected heart flutterings. "Bert, put me down! What would people say if they saw you doing that?"

"Pure unadulterated joy, lady. Your little ship is finally turning in the tide." He said grinning widely. "Let's go downstairs for lunch under the oak tree and wait for Lucarelli to come in. Can't wait to see his face when you show him what you've discovered."

The two best friends had just gone downstairs with their packed sandwiches when Lucarelli's unmarked car pulled in the driveway and seeing them sitting on the table outside, walked over and joined them.

"Sit still and eat your lunch. I've had mine at the local Burger King. You can fill me in what you've just discovered while you stuff your mouths."

Maggie proceeded to fill him in, not only with Denny's discovery in the outlaying field, but also about the honeycomb and the azalea tree. "Is Denny still here, Maggie? I'd like to talk to him, also to the volunteer…what's her name? Connie?"

"Yes, of course. I asked them both to be available a little longer if you needed to talk to them. Denny is by
188

the entrance to the museum corralling the beehive and Connie is indoors, probably leading a tour or something. She's on duty until three."

"I think I'll take my chances with Connie first and let Denny finish with the beehive", Lucarelli decided wisely since he didn't know if bee bites were covered by his police insurance.

"I'll meet you inside after I talk to Connie. I'd like to see the knife Denny found first before I talk to him."

"Knife? What knife?" Bert wanted to know. Maggie briefed him apologizing for not having had the time to tell him the good news before Lucarelli arrived.

"Well, well!" Bert whistled in admiration. "You sure must have friends in very high places, Maggie, have you been saying your prayers?"

"OF COURSE, I've been saying my prayers, Bert Lincoln. Our dear Lord knows that little old ladies my age can't take too many more surprises", she said grinning broadly and playfully punching his arm. "Now hurry up and eat your sandwich so we can go upstairs."

"I see you left part of yours Is it O.K. if I have it?"

"Sure thing, piggy-piggy" demonstrated Maggie making a face at him. "Better hurry. I'm going to tell Denny that Lucarelli is here in case he's not through with the bees. When you're through eating, just come to my office."

"Be right there, Boss Lady!" said Bert impudently stuffing his mouth with Maggie's left over sandwich.

Twenty minutes later, Lucarelli knocked at Maggie's office door and entered. "Spoke to the young lady volunteer about the tea that Jeff served Mrs. Cartwright. Wish we had known this before and saved everyone a ton of worry. Now show me what Denny found in the field. "

"Mind if Bert comes along to the next room, with us Luke? He's a member of the board and I need someone to corroborate the finding before we meet later."

Maggie stuck her head in the secretary's room and asked that they not be disturbed for the next twenty minutes or so, and if Denny came up, to please wait for them in her office. Amy nodded and continued her typing.

The trio walked into Jeff's workroom where the refrigerator, which had been emptied after Jeff's murder, now contained the probable murder weapon. Maggie took out the newspaper wrapped object and laid on Jeff's worktable, thinking how fitting it was to be there to try and uncover his murderer. Lucarelli snapped on a pair of rubber gloves he always carried in his jacket pocket, and carefully opened the wrapped newspaper.

"Hmm. Lethal weapon all right. The kind the Mafia people use in Chicago and New York. The rusty stains are blood that will be matched against some of the blood spatters from the deceased recovered by the lab techs here. By all first looks though, it appears your guy Denny just had a major find in that field. I'll need to talk to him and have him show me where exactly he found it. Probably discarded by the killer. Wouldn't do to be found with blood stains on your dinner jacket."

 When he said that, both Bert and Maggie exchanged looks. "You're thinking it was someone HERE that killed Jeff?"

 "Right now, it's only a possibility and I will ask that you do not discuss this with anyone until tests have been run. The blood stains and the knife stains have to be compared. Given the type of weapon, it does suggest the type of individual here who could have wielded it with that kind of brutal efficiency and then discarded it, so as not to focus attention on him here. Now show me the box where Jeff's tea things are and I can also take it and see if there are traces of the poison found in either the tea things or the honey."

 "I know where we have empty boxes in the museum, " Bert volunteered. "We save all the cardboard that may be reused again. That's part of my volunteer duties when I'm here." Saying this he exited hurriedly, telling them that Denny was waiting in Maggie's office to speak to the detective.

 Denny had brought the honeycomb Maggie had requested from the beehive, and had wrapped it up securely in some aluminum foil. Lucarelli accepted the wrapped object and placed it in the box containing Jeff's tea things, telling Maggie he was going to ask the lab to look and see if there were some of the Azalea poison traces in the honey from that particular honeycomb. "I'm going down with Denny to look at the site where he found the stiletto," he said to Maggie and Bert who had returned with an appropriate box to place the knife still wrapped with the newspapers that Denny had used. "By the way, I'm staying nearby in the Vermont Barracks and will be back here tomorrow for Jeff's funeral. I'm interested on who is going to show."

 Lucarelli deftly gathered the boxes with Jeff's tea things and the one with the murder weapon, and waved goodbye to Maggie and Bert. "See you tomorrow…and Maggie: thanks! You've made my job a hell of a lot easier." He winked at her and went downstairs followed by Denny. He deposited the boxes in the trunk of his car and drove Denny to the field next to the parking area where the stiletto had been found.

 Bert said, "I'm going to call Samantha and tell her that there are new findings in the case of Jeff's murder. I'll mention that Lucarelli does not want to divulge at this time some of the findings and that it would be best to postpone the board meeting a little while until more facts can be disclosed to the board."

"Thanks, Bert! That's a great load of my mind."

192

Bert hesitated momentarily, then reached across Maggie's desk for a half hug and planted a gentle kiss on her forehead. "Totally, my very great pleasure to be of assistance to a damsel in distress, Mrs. Maggie Winters. Want a ride to the funeral? I think you'll need a friend at your side." Maggie nodded her agreement dumbly. He gave her his customary wink and was off. The sound of his sports car was heard roaring down the hill a few minutes later.

CHAPTER TWENTY TWO

Samantha Vanderpool had made arrangements to meet Lester and the museum's pro bono attorney Rick Dupreville, a highly respected New Hampshire and Vermont attorney, for lunch at one. Ronnie Santini, one of the new board members owned a very popular Italian restaurant nearby and offered to pick up the lunch tab at his restaurant. Rick had been one of the top prosecutors in New Hampshire and after a stint as State Attorney General, he had left politics for private practice and was generous with non-profit entities that might require legal counsel.

Rick arrived first and hurried to the booth where Samantha had been sipping a glass of white wine while she awaited her two guests. He had been briefed over the phone when she issued the lunch invitation of what they could expect from the other attendee and the legal issues she was afraid he might bring against the little museum.

Lester arrived a few minutes later attired in a black Italian custom fit suit with a silver and gold tie. The effect was startling and emphasized his dark hooded eyes that darted around the room to "get the lay of the land" and where the exits were located.

"Sorry I was delayed at the mortuary. Who's this guy?" he asked abruptly gesturing in the vicinity of Rick. The attorney stood to greet him and handed him his card.

"I am counsel for the museum, Mr. Wonkrowski, and am here to assist Mrs. Vanderpool with any concerns you may have. Rick inspected Les' s face and for a brief instant his brows knit in concentration, but continued, "Of course we're very sorry for your loss and offer our deepest sympathy and condolences."

"I just worked for Prudence. She was nothing personal to me", was the brusque response. "For the time being I'm taking over management of the galleries until the family selects a new director."

"Galleries?" was Rick's question.

"New York and Chicago."

The conversation stopped when Ronnie Santini approached the table and asked what everybody was drinking. He took the drink orders and brought them back along with a menu of Italian specialty dishes.

"You Italian so I can recommend a specialty?" Ronnie asked Lester.

"Mother was Sicilian," was the brief reply.

"I can recommend the *Pasta alla Norma, Involtini di Pesce Spada* and *Impanata di Pesce Spada.*"

"Enough, already. Bring whatever won't take all day. I have to be back in Chicago this afternoon with the ashes so that her adult kids can have a funeral for their mother. They live in Illinois and run the gallery there. Now take the other orders and go get it done."

Samantha, to her credit, felt necessary to mention that Mr. Santini was a member of the museum board and should be given the courtesy of his position.

"Whatever." was the sole reply.

Lester continued without waiting for any response, "Let's get down to business here, people. I got the report from the police that the death was caused by a blow to the head and I want to know who's got responsibility here. This rinky-dink museum can't exist with bad publicity, and believe me, I can make it hard for you. IF I want to."

"What would make you even **remotely** think that someone in this museum would be interested in doing away with a generous donor like Mrs. Cartwright in such a violent manner? It would seem to me an art dealer with her reputation for ruthlessness would have made a lot of enemies either in New York or Chicago. I would warrant there are more vengeful mobsters there than what we have here. Before you start making unfounded accusations against this museum, I strongly suggest that you think before you speak, Mr.

Wonkrowski," was Rick's cool and instant reply.

"What about the old dame who still directs this so-called museum? She had a reason to dislike Prudence who recommended to your president here that she ought to be replaced with someone younger and not so set on her ways."

"The director of this museum has been a highly respected member of the New England Arts Commission. Her supporters nationwide include collectors and donors of Parrish and other members of the Cornish Colony such as the members of the Gertrude Vanderbilt Whitney family in New York, the Du Ponts of Delaware, the major lights in today's computer world like Jobs, Gates,...."

Rick was interrupted abruptly. "Don't care who you have as 'friends' and 'donors'. What's important is that Prudence is gone and the heirs want some kind of tit for tat since it happened here".

"In other words, you're trying to shake the museum down, are you Lester?"

"Don't care what you call it. The Family wants some kind of retribution, like the gift of a painting similar to the one that was so called 'stolen'. I bet the old dame hid it somewhere until all this died down. Anyway, I'm done here. Said what I wanted to say." Les pushed away the table upsetting his chair as he stood up. "You'll be hearing again from me or our attorneys and it won't be pretty," he said wadding his linen napkin and slamming on the table. The restaurant had gone silent watching the tantrum display from the Chicago native as he walked towards the entrance and slammed the door behind him.

Rick apologized to Samantha saying this was not what he had hoped would happen. His brow furrowed, the former Attorney General thought back. "I've seen that face and those narrow eyes before in some mug shot from the Chicago area. Let me look into that before this gets out of hand, Samantha. Let's salvage the rest of the meal that's coming up. Looking forward to the Sicilian dishes we ordered. I promise to make some calls when I get back to my office and find out a little bit more about our unsavory luncheon guest in the time it takes him to fly back to Chicago."

Samantha, still shell-shocked from the bombastic display from Lester, was not able to manage a good showing for the delicacies Ronnie Santini had set before them. "Don't forget Jeff's funeral tomorrow, Rick! It'll be at St. Francis. I would appreciate your presence there."

"Planning on it, Samantha. I'll share what I find with you after the funeral."

The next day dawned overcast and traces of drizzle were apparent when Maggie peered out her kitchen window while she was preparing her morning cup of decaffeinated. Somehow, again, Mother Nature seemed to mirror the sadness of what the day would bring during the funeral of her friend.

She dressed somberly in a dark pantsuit with a white silk blouse and accessorized herself with her mother's string of pearls and single pearl earrings. Since the museum was going to be closed, she had more time in the morning that she usually did, so she was ready when Bert Lincoln pulled up in his little sports car, which in deference to the occasion, had its top in place. The two friends drove almost silently to St. Francis Church and parked in the back lot that strategically faced the church's main entrance to accommodate parishioners who braved the cold blasts of winter and mounds of snow.

The closed casket was borne solemnly in, and Maggie noted happily that Denny Grant and a couple of the museum's male board of directors had been asked to be the pallbearers. She was glad that Jeff's "friends and museum family" participated in transporting his casket. Since Jeff was an only child to his now very elderly parents, it was natural that the sight of his casket caused both of them to clutch at each other and collapse in tears of grief.

Maggie and Bert who were seated directly behind them, went around to the first pew and embraced them in sober commiseration of their unspeakable loss. Maggie had been asked to offer some thoughts about Jeff's work at the museum and his loyal and unquestioning love for the art under his care as conservator and installation specialist. After Mass, the officiating priest incensed the casket and as the congregation sang a traditional hymn:

"And He will raise you up on Eagles' wings,

Bear you on the breath of dawn,

Make you to shine like the sun

And hold you in the palm of His hands".

One by one the cars of people in the full church who had known and appreciated Jeff and loved the devotion which he had always had for the art, followed the hearse silently to the cemetery where the casket was gently lowered after receiving the final blessing from the officiating priest who came over to comfort the distraught parents of their only child.

When people were headed back to their cars, Lucarelli caught up with Maggie and Bert. "You two headed back to the museum? I have something of great interest to tell you. See you back there in fifteen minutes or so? I don't have much time. Have to head back to Montpelier."

Maggie had just time to turn off the alarms and turn on the lights when some of the other staff people came in as well as the volunteers on duty for the day. Everyone headed for their respective offices or places of duty and the hum of the museum resounded again as soon as the first visitors began trickling in.

Lucarelli arrived a few minutes later and headed straight into Maggie's office where she and Bert awaited anxiously what he had to say. Without wasting time, Detective Lucarelli began right in with

200

his narrative.

"Among the things the pathologist had found in doing an examination of Jeff's body was that the blade, probably a sharp stiletto knife had been used by a left handed killer because the cut from behind was a quick slice from right to left which signaled the user was a leftie. The knife found by Denny yesterday had an extremely narrow blade similar to the one thought to be the murder weapon. These appear to be the 'silent weapon' of choice for many of the Italian mafia henchmen."

"The weapon discovered in the adjacent field is a standard BUDK 'Kissing Crane' burnt bone Damascus steel folding knife. They're slim and hard to detect when hidden in the inside pocket of a man's suit or in his trouser's pants. Now we have the weapon the killer discarded probably because of the blood in the blade. I can see him tossing it to the nearby field when he left the house and probably mingled with the people loading the ambulance with Mrs. Cartwright's body. We have not let it be known the pathologist's theory that the killer was a left handed man. We are keeping our eyes open and running queries in the databases for left handed killers."

"He may have been a guest, or he may have been someone who took advantage of the commotion in the parking lot to kill Jeff while everyone else was busy being onlookers. We still do not have a motive for Jeff's killing unless he surprised the killer after the painting was removed. Jeff had just dialed 911 when the killer came up from behind and killed him. We logged a call from his number but when it was answered there was no one on the line. We are looking at the possibility of gathering other clues as to the profile of the killer. Perhaps an earlier print left on the knife handle by its owner at another time might be discovered. We know the killer here wore examination rubber gloves and then probably discarded them so as not to appear in public with tell-tale bloody hands."

There was stunned silence in the room. "Obviously, this information is not to be disseminated to anyone else yet, or we might lose our man," Lucarelli added almost as an afterthought. "I need you to be alert to left handed people that were either attendees at the party or that you know about in relationship with the museum. Again, please let me reiterate: do not discuss this with anyone. That's why I wanted the two of you together so one would not be tempted to tell the other."

Standing and stretching his aching back, Lucarelli informed the pair he needed to get back to Montpelier and see if there were any hits in the police computer on the one print found earlier at the museum's entryway where someone had discarded heavy, mud covered boots before silently making his way in the museum.

The two friends remained at their places unable to absorb the information they had been given. It seemed too much to take in at the time, right after Jeff's funeral.

"Oh, Bert! I can't seem to take it all in. My head is literally spinning."

"It's probably your blood pressure, Maggie. Sit still here at your desk while I rummage around for a cup of your favorite tea."

"You know my favorite tea, do you?"

"Everyone knows your favorite tea is chamomile, Maggie. Or at least it has been your favorite since we met some years ago when I was inducted into the museum board of directors. I notice these things." He left her still sitting unmoving at her desk and went into the staff break room to see what was available.

The rest of the week went by fast, Maggie feeling as if she were transported to a different dimension when the expected things turned out to be wrong or unfamiliar.

Over and over she reviewed the events of that fateful Lender's and Donor's Dinner.

She played in her mind the last minutes she had with Jeff together turning off the lights in the exhibit space and how he had urged her to go on ahead and join the guests while he finished turning off the lights. He was usually so meticulous. Then, the thought of the *Dingleton* frame having been placed squarely back on its pencil marked site assaulted her memory. It was something so unusual for a robber to do, particularly if he were working in the dark. Jeff was sure to have turned off the lights before exiting the room after she left. Surely, no robber in his right mind would turn on lights while the museum was still full of people. He would be announcing his presence, for Heaven's sake!

The fact that the frame was left behind made sense, since it would have been too bulky to be removed unnoticed. All a person had to do was turn the simple butterfly wings the artist had installed in the frame and the little oil on board would pop out. Since the board was only a few millimeters thick, it could easily be hidden under whatever the robber was wearing.

But who knew how simply it was attached? Museums did not normally show the backs of their art works to visitors. Many times, the well known works showed the lender's name on the back or in what other museums it had been, besides who would have known how Mr. Parrish had attached it to its frame unless they had been shown by a member of the museum staff.

"Oh, no!", Maggie thought horrified at the memory. "I showed the back of the painting to Prudence Cartwright the day she visited. She ASKED me to see the back, and I acted impulsively in obliging her, seeing as she had just made a donation to the museum to cover the insurance on the new acquisition. She saw how Mr. Parrish had attached it and knew it would be easy to take it off the frame with a few flicks of the wrist to turn the butterfly screws and release the board out of its frame. SHE KNEW!! She had wanted the painting for a client, and maybe since the museum would not sell it to her, could she have decided to find another way of getting it."

The realization made her sink back into her chair, a feeling of having let down the institution she so loved by her feelings of pride in the little work that had just been donated by her dear friend Dotty Granville. "I'm responsible for it being taken! I'm the one responsible for having lost it!!!" was her awful thought.

She sat still in a dazed state until her secretary tapped discreetly at the door and asked her if she wanted her to turn off the museum lights before leaving. Maggie nodded absently, and said, "Well, I guess I'm now the only one to turn the alarms on and off daily now that Jeff is gone…. Go ahead and turn off the lights, Amy. I'll be leaving shortly too. It's been a very difficult day!"

"I can see that, Maggie. Go home, take a hot bath and do something kind for yourself like a hot toddy or a cup of hot chocolate! Goodnight!"

Dejectedly, Maggie gathered her purse, turned off the office lights and descended the long stairway only by the light of the Emergency sign by the door. She automatically armed the alarm and closed the locked door, heading straight for her little Subaru and home.

CHAPTER TWENTY THREE

When she got home, Maggie dispiritedly walked in and turned on the light switch. What she saw to her horrified amazement was total chaos everywhere: kitchen cupboards open, bookshelves emptied, their contents scattered on the floor, the linen closets the same. Whoever had gone through looking for something seemingly had not found it and one could detect a certain amount of fury in the way objects, including the dirty clothes in the bathroom hamper lay scattered everywhere.

With trembling hands, she dialed 911 and called for help…then she dialed Bert, who thankfully was home watching a favorite sports channel. He said he would be right over. The police beat Bert to the door, but only just. Thank God they had not collided on the country road coming from opposite directions!

Unseemly or not, as soon as he arrived, Bert took her in his arm and held her tightly until the trembling stopped while she was trying to stammer her answers to the police officer from the station closest to her house.

After taking her name, age, place of employment and the initial report on the breaking and entering, the young policeman asked, "Do you know what this was about, Mrs. Winters? Looks as if someone appears to have a kind of grudge against you. Can you spot anything of value missing? Any disgruntled employees at the museum?" The young policeman who answered the 911 call asked respectfully.

While they were still talking , a second patrol car pulled in and Mike Walters, the Vermont police captain who had done the initial report on the apparent theft and the subsequent murder at the museum, walked in.

"Hi, Maggie! Heard on the police scanner that it was your cottage involved in the break in, so I decided to look in on you. Looks as if someone one had it in for you or was looking for something he thought you might have, seeing the way your place was disrupted. Any thoughts on that subject?"

Maggie dumbly just shook her head. It felt as if the whole room was spinning around her and was doubly grateful of Bert's strong presence by her side, still holding her somewhat steady.

"Look, do you have a place to stay tonight? I can come over to the museum tomorrow morning and talk to you when you're calmer after a good night's sleep. I was on duty at Jeff's funeral last week because we expected a crowd and weren't disappointed. You looked tired then and you look all in now. This little cottage is pretty much off the beaten path and you live alone so it might be better if you stay with friends tonight. Besides we want to dust for prints and hope that our guy here did not think to wear gloves to go through your stuff the way he threw things around."

Bert grinned at the officer and turning to Maggie he said, "You should see how much money I used on Mike to bribe him to say that to you. You heard it from the Captain's mouth. You're coming home with me whether you want to or not, maiden lady! I promised to be on my best behavior and my children's former rooms are all available to you. C'mon lady! Pack a small bag and let me whisk you away."

Maggie smiled gratefully. She had women friends she could call who would be delighted to have her stay with them, but staying with Bert would be even more comforting. "Go ahead with the guy, Maggie. My lips are sealed and I promised not to blab to your friends about where you'll stay tonight, " Mike Walters smiled and continued. "That way only I know where you'll be and your reputation will be intact."

Maggie decided that she would feel infinitely safer if she stayed with Bert in his home across the Connecticut River. She packed a bag quickly and efficiently, made sure her laptop was with her and went home with him across the 150+ year covered bridge that joined Windsor, VT with Cornish, NH on the other side. She left her Subaru at home so that people would think she was still there and all was well.

The smell of bacon and eggs on the grill as well as the wonderful odor of good strong coffee alerted her senses that she was not home since the stuff she was sniffing was coming from the kitchen and she was still in bed. She stretched luxuriously, or as luxuriously as a 70+ year old body would let her, wiggled her toes and fingers to see if everything was still working, said some quick prayers and slid out of the big queen size bed.

After a quick shower and shampoo of her short white curly hair, she dressed quickly in tan pants and a nice Talbot's pullover and after making her bed, she hurried down to the kitchen. Bert's country kitchen had a luxuriously large window that reflected the perfectly mowed meadow behind his house. Many a times she had been here when it was Bert's turn to host a get-together for the board and had seen moose and deer quietly munching close to the denser undergrowth of the next field. Bert liked fishing because it was a solitary, quiet time for him away from ringing phones and other pressing activities of his retirement world such as his commitments to the museum and his service on the board of Selectmen for the town of Cornish. He did not like hunting and preferred to enjoy the safety that his acres would provide the local wild life because of his posted "NO HUNTING" signs on his property.

"Sleep well, lady?" was Bert's teasing remark to his friend.

"Very well, thank you, kind sir! Gee, Bert, I was so glad to see you come in the cottage after finding it in such havoc. I haven't properly thanked you, yet."

"Yes, you have, Maggie, by your willingness to come to my humble abode and risk the gossip mongers of both towns."

"Yes, there's that, but somehow, in the bigger scheme of things I don't really give a fig about it right now."

"Good girl! These dangerous and risky situations you have recently experienced certainly put the emphasis on what is important and what's not. Girl, you're growing up in front of my very eyes," he said teasingly.

" I think I'm done growing UP, Bert. I am growing DOWN while you seem to be growing lankier and taller. " Both friends smiled and he gestured for her to sit down and have her first cup of NON-decaffeinated coffee in a long time. "Now, I'm pouring you a cup of truth serum. Tell me what you think of the latest goings on, how I can be of help to you, and where you think this is going in the future. You know that two heads are always better than one."

"It depends on which two heads we're talking about, Bert, " Maggie said smiling broadly. With that said, she launched on a recitations of all the thoughts that had been troubling her, beginning with seeing the empty *Dingleton* frame hanging precisely between the four pencil marks Jeff had made during the Installation to indicate how exactly the painting should be hung.

She ended with the latest event of the trashing of her house by someone who was evidently attempting to find a hidden object in her place or simply to show malice towards her.

"Maggie, did it even occur to you that Jeff took the little painting upstairs before locking up the room and turning out the lights?"

"It did occur to me, Bert. But, why? We looked for it, obviously, and went into the vault and it was not in the place where we would store the museum owned art works. As you know, there is a demarcation line on the vault. The things on the right belong to lenders of the exhibit. The things on the left (where our heart is sited) belong to the museum. Jeff came up with that placement and I went along with how he wanted to store the objects that needed returning at the end of the exhibit as opposed to the things that did not need wrapping or boxing and were simply stored in the vertical shelves standing upright with large sheets of cardboard between them so as not to mar the patina on the frames. We save all the boxes of the works shipped to us on loan and use them to return back to the original lenders. That saves the museum from unnecessary expenses as well as being good for the environment."

"All well and good, Maggie. But I had heard from Samantha Vanderpool earlier yesterday that her lunch with Lester and our attorney did not go well. I gathered that Lester seemed to think that the museum had hidden the painting and that *Dingleton* was still in our possession. He then intimated that if it was 'found' he would want it given or sold cheaply to his gallery so they could sell it to that cheesy Chicago client Mr. Jones. Otherwise the implied threat was an accusation of Wrongful Death against the museum."

"Well, instead of driving me home, why don't we drive straight to the museum and both of us go through the vault together to see if we find anything of interest there that Jeff may have wanted to safeguard against these thieves."

"That's the best idea you've come up with so far, Maggie"

"And the day is just beginning, Bert. Give me time to digest this really good coffee and breakfast and see if my little grey cells get a power boost from them."

"Now you're thinking," said Bert agreeably beginning to gather the dishes and dumping them in the sink.

When Detective Lucarelli arrived at his desk in Montpelier, there were several messages for him including one asking him to call the FBI office in New York. He dialed the number given and got Special Agent Dyer. The agent, a specialist in the fingerprint section, told him that the print which Vermont had sent them had a match. This was the print Lucarelli's men had lifted off the museum portico near where the intruder with the muddy boots had left on the day *Dingleton* had disappeared.

The print belonged to a body dragged out of the water at a New Jersey waterfront pier whose name was Vito Lipinski, a small time crook who was known to be a break in specialist with some knowledge of alarms. They had found a car with no registration left abandoned at the pier that had presumably belonged to Mr. Lipinski. But, best of all, they found a cudgel tucked under the driver's seat (as if someone in a huge hurry had tossed it in upon entering the car). They checked the prints on the cudgel to their database and came up with the same match: Lipinski. The cudgel's thick end had some faint smudges of blood and long strands of synthetic hair such as may have come from a woman's wig.

"BINGO!" Lucarelli yelled into the phone causing several heads in his department to look up and grin at him, and he knew he was in for some jokester asking him if he had scored big in the Parish's Thursday Bingo Game night.

"That's very helpful, Agent Dyer. Was the dead body autopsied or did he drown naturally?"

"He drowned, all right probably in his own blood. His throat had been slit from ear to ear with a very sharp rapier."

"Bingo again! Now we're getting somewhere! My department is currently analyzing a similar death and my guys are matching the blood on a blade we found last week at the crime scene with spatters on it.. I will make sure you're copied with the report. Maybe it might be the same type of blade that did the deed there."

"Sure, send the report and we'll copy the New York Police Department for their files on Lipinski. Make sure you keep us in the loop. Any prints on that blade?" the FBI Agent added hopefully.

"No. The killer here wore gloves."

"Bummer!" was the reply before Agent Dyer hung up the phone.

When Maggie and Bert arrived at the museum, they saw Denny already out with his crew working on the grounds. Denny came up to the car and said to Maggie, "Heard what happened at your place on the Police Scanner, Maggie! Wanted to tell you that my wife and I are very sorry for your loss. I drove by early this morning to see if you needed anything since your car was still there, but I see you were in good hands here with Bert," Denny said smiling widely.

"Nothing more than any other good friend would do and I was the nearest one when she called. You have a scanner?"

"Shhh! Don't tell anyone. They're not really allowed but since I'm on the Volunteer Fire Department I carry it so I know when I'm needed. By the way, Maggie, the Mrs asked me to tell you that if it's all right with you, she'll go in with a couple of ladies and clean it up before the end of the day so that you don't have to look at it. It will be our pleasure."

"Spoilsport!" was Bert's only comment, his eyes however smiling at the kindness being proffered to his friend.

Maggie who had been blushing red since Denny's earlier knowledge of her staying with Bert, smiled at him and said, "It would be very gracious of the two of you and I can't keep imposing on Bert for another overnight."

"Yes, you can and you know it, lady! Anyway turn off the darn alarm and let's get to work on today's assignment" was Bert's reply.

Since Denny was on Maggie's side of the car, he opened the door for her. As she walked ahead, Bert whispered to Denny: "Keep a look out for her Denny. She lives so alone and apart from people, and we're dealing with not-so-nice individuals here lately."

"I always tell her I have her back, Bert" was the hefty grounds keeper's comment.

A few minutes later, the museum was once again ablaze with lights as the first visitors of the day as well as staff and volunteers arrived. It had a life of its own and Maggie vowed she would do anything in her power to keep it going as long as she could.

The director gave instructions to her small staff to keep alert and that she and Bert Lincoln were going to go through the vault again and did not wish to be disturbed.

Meticulously they searched the bins painting by painting in the section of the works owned by the museum or any other logical place Jeff would have chosen to safeguard *Dingleton* overnight in case he was the one that had placed it back inside the safe. After a solid hour and a half of backbreaking work moving crates and precious art objects from side to side searching for a little unframed 12"x 16"oil painted on a board that was only about 10mm thick, they decided to take a break.

Bert contemplated, "Would Jeff have stored it in the other side, where the works owned by others are stored. We would have to open all the boxes and crates where the art objects were shipped to us that we just put back in the vault."

"Let's review the happenings on that night. The owners and donors had just been summoned to the dining room by the ringing of the chimes at 8:00 pm. Jeff and I stayed behind to ascertain that the exhibition rooms were vacant of all visitors and stragglers. After that he shooed me back out to join our guests. *Dingleton* was on the wall when I left the room, at the most five minutes later. I arrived and the toasts were just being made, then the cold soup was served. Let's say a total of ten more minutes perhaps when Jeff arrived and took his place. His soup was still there and they were serving the salad."

Maggie continued the train of thought, "OK, so he

had a total of no more than 20 minutes tops, to take the oil on board down, turn the butterfly screws rapidly, return the empty frame to its exact spot as would have been his instinct, turn off the lights, lock the room, scoot upstairs, open the safe and put the painting somewhere easy to reach but out of sight and then sit down for the meal with the rest of the guests."

"O.K. Maggie. Let's go with the assumption that it was Jeff who removed the painting for safekeeping overnight. Maybe he might have overheard a conversation between Les and the Mr. Jones that made him uneasy or alarmed him about the safety of the work. He was proven right by the evident break-in to the exhibit room, hopefully, after Jeff had wisely transported *Dingleton* upstairs. The meticulous placing of the frame back in the wall points more to Jeff being the one to have placed it there. He didn't have too much time to spend upstairs before he had to be down in the dining room. Remember he had to open safe."

"Then let's say, he double steps upstairs, puts in the code, opens the safe, and places the work in an accessible spot that doesn't involve his having to cut cardboard to the dimensions of the little painting. He simply slips it down into an existing box, closes the safe's door, spins the dial to lock it, and then double steps it to the dining room and makes it down in time to get to his place when the salad is being brought out. Does that make sense?"

Maggie was silent for a brief moment then lifting a radiant face to meet his, she said: "I think you're absolutely right, Bert. I KNOW Jeff put the painting somewhere in a place that was completely logical to him! All we have to do is figure that out."

The phone in Detective Lucarelli's car buzzed while he was in his car driving. He put the call on speaker. "Lucarelli."

"Luke, this is Special Agent Dyer in New York. What was the date of the murder at your museum?"

"Let me think a second, I'm driving and don't have my notes handy. It was the night of the museum's Donor Banquet on Saturday near two weeks ago. "

"Bummer. The murder here was four days ago, so it could not have been the same blade since it was discarded there and is currently being analyzed by your guys. You said it was a stiletto knife? Our pathologist thinks the killer here was a lefty and he used a new, very sharp knife. Our Crime Scene people tell me it possibly may have been a stiletto, too. Some guys have a distinctive 'modus operandi' and they like using the same type of weapon over and over. I'll know more later. Have your lab send me the photo and the make of the knife and we'll compare it with what we have here."

"Thanks, Agent Dyer. I'll have them do that today."

Within a couple of hours that afternoon both police labs had exchanged information and found that both
218

knives were the same make and model. They had a
match.

Several miles down the road from the museum,
Denny's wife and a couple of volunteer friends were
just emerging from a day of straightening out Maggie's
cottage and as they walked to their cars, an expensive
car with a New York registration, which was just
starting up the road, saw the group headed for their
cars, and immediately reversed, and sped off leaving a
trail of rubber behind. Denny's wife immediately dialed
her husband's cell phone, told him of the event which
caused Denny to immediately turn off the tractor with
which was mowing the museum's lawn, and run to the
museum to alert Maggie.

Maggie and Bert were just on their way back upstairs
to check on her hunch of where the little *Dingleton*
might have been left, when a winded Denny stomped
into the entry way sweaty, and smelling as if he could
use a good long cool shower.

"Maggie, wait up, dear. Come down just a second. I
need to tell you something and I'm too winded to make
it up the stairs to your office."

Bert and Maggie looked at Denny's sunburned and
perspiring face and they both turned on their heels and
came down to see what the problem was. Maggie
suggested they go sit a spell at the table under the oak
where she and Bert had just finished their lunch. That
way, docent volunteers and visitors would not be
disturbed.

Denny took a few breaths and began by turning to Bert and saying, "Hey, Bert, how would you like to host Maggie a little longer at your place?"

"I'd love to Denny, but that's up to Maggie. What's up?"

"My wife and a couple of friends had just finished straightening Maggie's cottage and had it all spic and span. As they were leaving, a big Chrysler Town Car with New York plates had just turned onto her driveway and was heading up, when it saw the other cars and it did a screeching reverse and left leaving rubber behind."

"Denny, you know New York licenses are quite common during tourist season in Vermont and New England. I bet if you look at our museum parking lot right now, I bet you'll find one or two there. Maybe someone just took a wrong turn coming to the museum, realized they were in a private driveway and then, drove out."

"No, Maggie. I saw the same town car in our parking lot that Saturday during the Donor's Party. It had parked at the edge of the parking area near where Mrs. Cartwright parked her car. Wasn't that her associate that had driven in that fat guy from Chicago? I never liked the looks of either of them!"

Maggie felt a cold prickle of fear down her spine. Her keen sixth sense seemed to be on high alert. She remembered feeling that sense of dread when she had first felt when her little cottage had been thrashed. Unbidden, the words from <u>Macbeth</u> assaulted her mind:

> *'By the pricking of my thumbs,*
>
> *Something wicked this way comes.*
>
> *Open locks,*
>
> *Whoever knocks!'* [4]

"Thanks, Denny! I owe you one! I won't let this lady out of my sight for the next day or two or until this is resolved," was Bert's quick reply.

"I'm alerting my buddies in the police department and at the dispatchers to be on the lookout for this kind of big car. They sure stand out here in the sticks, don't they?" Denny quipped, feeling that Maggie was going to be fine if Bert kept her eye on her.

Sensing more than seeing it, Bert felt that Maggie's mind need to be engaged in a more positive course. "Let's go finish what we were going to look at upstairs, Maggie. Between Denny and the police our 'bad guy' doesn't have a chance! Besides, I've been waiting for a long time to be more of a presence in your life and somebody upstairs must have just sent me a very special gift!"

---

[4] Shakespeare, William. <u>Macbeth</u> Act 4, scene1, 44-49

Maggie accepted without a word, and after patting Denny's hand, she headed upstairs, the words of the Twenty Third Psalm echoing wordlessly in her head.

"Quick detour into the staff room for some chamomile tea and a cookie?" she asked Bert.

"You mention 'cookie' and I'm there, alert and willing," was Bert's reply. After their tea and cookies and while Maggie took a bathroom break, Bert pulled out his cell phone and made a couple of quick calls. Then they both headed for the room where the vault was located.

Upon entering Maggie asked Bert to give her a minute to walk through a possible scenario that she had been thinking about. They sat in a pair of easy chairs facing the massive vault that took up most of the wall on the side of the house where it had been sited over 100 years before.

"That puppy must have been brought up piece by piece and then assembled on site," mused Bert.

"What I DO know is that the owners previous to the museum had to do major architectural renovations before they could move in. The vault's weight had begun to buckle the entire floor and that had to be addressed by adding some steel girders below it and re-doing the entire floor above what at one time had been their ballroom and is now one of the main exhibit spaces. The museum architect had to give us assurances that the paintings would be safe when on display below before the recently formed non-profit board bought the place for the museum organization," was Maggie's comment.

Then she continued mulling her thoughts into some form of cohesive transition.

"This is what I think may have been Jeff's way of thinking: Remember he was a neat- nick and a fanatic for putting things and objects in the correct place. That's what made him invaluable to us as our Installer of Museum Exhibitions. He had extracted the oil on board out of its frame and then placed it back in its exact spot. Now he hurried up the stairs after carefully locking the exhibit space, and headed for the vault and opened it. The normal thing for him to do was to place it on the right side of the vault among the items owned by the museum. He realized that I insist each item be secured and separated from others by a labeled and acid free piece of cardboard on each side. He had no time to go out and locate a couple of boards, so what does he do?"

"I don't know. You tell me," was Bert's response.

"He goes to the left wall that holds all the empty packing boxes of the incoming loans which are now hanging downstairs, he pulls out the packing case where my friend Dotty Granville had sent us *Dingleton*, he lifts the lid and slips the painting between the acid free cardboard sheets which secured the work which was sent to us. It HAS to be there! These are arranged by size with the largest boxes being against the wall of the vault. We need to find a smaller box towards the beginning that is coming to us from Dorothea Granville in Carmel, California."

"O.K. Let's see if you're right."

Maggie said a quick inner prayer and added a P.S. to Jeff. "If you can hear us, Jeff, please show us that this is what you did."

With trembling hands, Maggie re-opened the mammoth vault door and walked to the left side of the vault where the other Owner's art was stored and where now the empty boxes awaited until the end of the exhibit to be returned to their owners. There were three small boxes in the front. Maggie went directly to the one that she knew had come from her friend, lifted the flap and peered inside.

"*Dingleton* is here, Bert!!!!! Just where Jeff left it! BLESSED BE GOD!"

CHAPTER TWENTY FOUR

Detective Lucarelli received a text message while he was headed back to work after a quick lunch break from the Vermont Police Barracks, informing him that the museum had located the *Dingleton Farm* painting which had been stored in a hidden place inside the vault by the technician who had been murdered. It asked him to get in touch with the museum's director so that she could and bring him up to date with some information he should know.

When Lucarelli got to his desk to look up the museum number, there were four waiting messages for him from Special Agent Dyer asking him to give him a call. "When you're HOT, you're HOT!" was Luke's take on his current popularity. He called Maggie first since her call had come in earlier.

The museum director sounded as if her voice were on edge and also brimming with excitement.

"They left a message for you that we found the painting Jeff had secured in a place that would not be obvious when the safe was open, but it is here and safe,

225

Luke. The thing that is most evident to those of us who work here was that Jeff was making sure that only the personnel that work in the museum would find it. It would not have been evident to a casual observer or to someone who might have attempted to break into the safe. I just KNOW Jeff must have overhead someone talking about arrangements being made for someone to come in and lift the painting while the dinner was in progress. So he went and took it out of its frame, hid it in the vault and then came downstairs to join the rest of the assembled guests for dinner. As we were finding the body of Mrs. Cartwright in the parking lot, he must have gone back upstairs to call the police to relate what he had overheard a couple of the guests say during the tea and cocktail party. I think one of those guests saw him going to his office and followed him upstairs with the intention of silencing him before he made the call. As a matter of fact, phone records for the local police indicate that a second 911 call had been made from a museum number but the caller hung up before he could say anything."

"One of the guests or his cold-blooded killer, Maggie. I think it may have been the latter. By the way, did you notice if any of your donors or lenders to the exhibit were left-handed?"

"Gosh, no, Luke. Not anyone I shook hands with, at least. But I can ask other museum personnel or advisory board members to see if anyone noticed a left handed person. But I did have something else to share with you that might be relevant to identifying the killer."

"I'm all ears, Maggie."

The director then told Lucarelli of the break in at her cottage the night before and the Chrysler Town Car with New York license plates that had been seen entering the driveway of her property and spotted by Denny's wife and the ladies who were straightening up the place.

"Don't go back there, Maggie. This guy whoever he is, IS dangerous. Stay with friends."

"I did last night and will do again for the next few evenings until this is solved, Luke. As you can probably tell, I'm a little out of kilter with all this going on at my age! Denny notified the local police and they're on the lookout for the car. Mighty conspicuous vehicle for this part of the country!"

"Good thinking, Maggie. I'll call your guy there, Mike Walters and ask him to be extra watchful. I assume the bad guy knows now we may be onto him so he will be extra dangerous to encounter. I think he'll ditch the big car and get out of town soon. I'll put the New York cops on alert and ask them if they know unsavory people with such a car and can give us something we can go on to trace the owner. Be sure to keep a low profile, hear?"

"Point taken Luke. Yes. I will be very careful and will be staying in the home of one of the board of directors."

They signed off and Lucarelli immediately dialed the FBI office in NY in response to their call. When he was put through to Special Agent Dyer's office, the FBI man immediately got to the subject at hand.

"We have a hit on the lefty killer. There are a couple of unsolved cases of people being killed with a stiletto knife both here in NY as well as one in Chicago. The killer was left handed AND used gloves so nothing was left to trace. The killer appears to be a cold-blooded bastard that thinks nothing of killing and may take some kind of pleasure in inflicting the kind of pain the victim will feel as he chokes in his own blood. It appears the cases have some ties to either the mob or to a boss who remains in the shadows and orders the hits. He moves around in the higher echelons, but is himself a well known killer among the people with whom he works. A dangerous and vindictive guy was what the pathologists seem to think because of the force of the initial thrust, usually in the same manner, with the victim's head tilted backward to expose the carotid vein to the blade. Death is almost instantaneous. We'll keep you posted on this."

"Thanks, Agent Dyer. Ditto with info from here", Lucarelli said, ending the call.

Denny had driven his wife and the two lady volunteers that had helped in cleaning out Maggie's cottage. He found out that the youngest of the volunteers, the one with the better eyesight, had caught a part of the Town

Car's New York license plate number. Mike Walters had encouraged them to come in and he'd see if there might be some hits in the database system on that distinctive car. Turns out there were!

Two weeks earlier the New Hampshire State Police had pulled over a Chrysler Town Car with an out-of-state license plate, proceeding east towards the Manchester airport and being obviously in a hurry to get there. The car was registered to the Cartwright Gallery of New York and the driver's license was in the name of a "Lester Wonkrowski", who identified himself as an employee of the gallery.

The all points bulletin alert for the car was issued and the particulars wired to both the Montpelier Barracks for Detective Lucarelli, and to the FBI and Special Agent Dyer in New York.

At the end of this especially exciting day, Maggie was driven by Bert home so that she could pack a suitcase with items and changes of clothing she might need in the next few days. Bert had made himself at home and opened a bottle of white wine Maggie had in the refrigerator and helped himself to a leisurely drink of the wine while the director fussed around in her bedroom gathering her things.

Suddenly alert, Bert sat up in the couch where he had chosen to sit, slouched low in it, taking in all the work the volunteers had done that day. He thought he had heard the crunch of tires against loose gravel and looked out to see what appeared to be one of the local trucks in the area approaching. Maybe a neighbor wanted to check that Maggie's place was all right after the break-in the day before. The truck swerved when it saw two cars in the driveway and disappeared from view. Bert thought that all the events of the past days not only had Maggie on high alert, but it also had him hyper sensitive to what was going on. Maggie came out to the living room holding the phone. "Something's wrong with the phone, Bert. I don't have a sound tone."

"Here, use my cell phone, Maggie. Who did you want to call? I'll dial it for you and pass it on." Bert knew well his friend's dislike for gadgetry and cell phones and anticipated her unfamiliarity with it.

"Just wanted to let my next door neighbor know that I'm taking the Subaru and spending a few days with friends until things calm down."

Maggie was still speaking when the front door opened silently and the brooding, hunched shoulders of Les Wonkrowski filled the entire doorway. "If I were you, I wouldn't be calling anyone now. It's a little too late for the two of you. Put the damn phone down. I just cut the lines anyhow so don't get any ideas. Let's you and I have a little talk before things get ugly."

Bert took a couple of steps towards Maggie evidently trying to protect her from the pointed gun the hit man was carrying. "Move back, Lancelot or whoever you are. I'm very handy with this little toy and as you can plainly see. It's outfitted with a silencer so as not to

230

disturb your neighbors in case I decide I need to shoot you," he smirked.

Maggie's voice had taken almost a calm tonality despite the desperate situation. It was always thus with her: calm during the storm and then dissolve into a puddle of nerves afterward. "I know what you're after, Les. You heard we found *Dingleton*, but it won't do you any good if you get rid of me since we took the precaution to keep it in the vault 'til all of this calms down. Since you killed the only other person who knew the combination, and you still have to get in the door past the alarm, it's me or nothing."

"Well, I like it when someone understands it like it is, but just in case, I'm keeping our friend here as insurance. If I don't get *Dingleton*, I'll fry him and this house on my way back. I took the precaution of cutting the phone lines and taking the air out of both of your vehicles tires."

Turning to Bert who was shooting him daggers with his eyes, Les motioned him to sit down on one of the kitchen chairs by pointing with his gun made longer by the addition of the silencer. He withdrew a blade from one of his pockets, and with a flick of his right hand, the stiletto opened silently, malignantly reflected in the light from the kitchen. The killer threw at Maggie some tough nylon rope he had carried in presumably from the weather beaten truck parked outside. "Tie him up with this, Maggie. No Mickey Mouse tricks or I hurt your boyfriend right in front of you."

Maggie's bravado could just take her so far and she felt herself starting to tremble. "Do as he says, Maggie. I'll be alright," Bert's soothing voice encouraged her to follow the orders. Neither of them had any hope of surviving this encounter but if they could just keep him from losing his cool and ending their lives before getting *Dingleton*, they were buying time for others to realize what was going on if the lights of the museum all of a sudden were turned on again. Where were the Vermont extra police people when you really needed them Maggie thought disconsolately.

Pointing his gun at them, he said: "Hurry up we haven't all day".

With trembling hands, Maggie had just started to wind the rope around Bert in the chair when with the corner of her eye, she saw a sturdy looming figure silhouetted against the front door, which suddenly slammed open as someone surprised them all by barging in. The next sound was a sickening thud of an iron garden wrench hitting with a great deal of force on Les' skull. The killer's gun went off with a small "SPLAT" sound when it hit the ground, opening a hole into the refrigerator door, and the deadly knife clattered harmlessly to the ground and lay besides the prone figure of the killer. Maggie hurried to kick it with her foot and send it clattering on the tile kitchen floor.

"If he makes it after that hit, he won't be all that dangerous for a long time to come" the genial but somewhat shaky voice of Denny sounded like the clarion call from the heaven's above to Maggie!

232

"Denny! How did you know? How blessed of you to be going by. Surely God's angels were watching after us if they sent you to help!"

"Maggie, you be sounding like my dear Irish mother, there must be some Irish in you! I was headed home past your place after stopping at the Hardware Store to pick up a brand new garden wrench, when I saw this disreputable looking truck coming from the opposite direction turn into your driveway with his lights out. Call me spooked, but I just knew the critter was up to no good, so I drove past and called you. When I got the signal that the line was disconnected, I doused my lights and came up. Saw the guy slashing your tires, so I got on the cell phone and called it in, then huffed up the rest of the way with only the new garden wrench in my hand as my weapon. I see that's all it took!"

Maggie swept her arms around Denny and started sobbing in relief. Bert had managed to untangle himself and he joined Maggie in embracing the gentle giant that was Denny Grant. Moments later the police lights and sirens once more made their wailing presence in the hill, this time the joyous clarion call of all things ending well that had somehow started so awfully wrong.

A few days later after all things had begun to be cleared up and understood by all concerned parties, Maggie returned to her little cottage once more, this time with feelings that life alone was not nearly as much fun as if there were someone you specifically cared about and whose presence made life around you infinitely sweeter and more enjoyable.

The very next evening, Bert convinced Maggie that there was some celebrating to be done at last. He announced that he was taking her out to dinner at one of the most beautiful and scenic of the Vermont restaurants situated in Quechee next to what at one time had been an old mill pond by the cascades that fed the turning water wheel which kept the mill going all those years. Parrish had created one of his scenic landscapes here and named it *The Mill Pond*.

Once seated next to the window in the picturesque restaurant watching the roar of the water over the rocks, the two friends held hands in a new found intimacy that each one seemed to enjoy. Maggie looked around and smiled. Bert wanted to know what she was thinking at that very precise moment...

"How beautiful everything appears, the moon reflected on the waters, the peaceful serene feeling of being with someone of whom you are very fond, the roar of the water against the rocks. And all of a sudden I remembered: Mr. Parrish did not name the little painting we just added to our inventory *Dingleton Farm*. That's the name that the publisher of the print for whom it was made gave to it. Mr. Parrish's name seems more fitting, particularly tonight."

"And the name of it, the envelope, please", teased Bert.

"You'd never guess it, but it's sure appropriate given

the serenity and the peaceful feeling I'm experiencing being here with you: Maxfield Parrish named it *Peace of Evening.*"

 "Well, he'd know, wouldn't he?" Bert smiled, taking her hand between his and raising it delicately to his lips.

END NOTES

The Maxfield Parrish painting *Dingleton Farm*, 1956, a small oil approximately 11"x 16" was actually owned by the author and was stolen from her San Francisco gallery on March 15, 1975. Miraculously, the painting resurfaced 30 years later. An auction gallery contacted her and asked if she was aware it was coming up for sale. After proving her ownership of the work and providing authorities with copies of her bill of sale dated in 1975, as well as the police report at the time of the theft and the subsequent newspaper articles on the theft, she finally recovered the work several months later, thirty years to the date when it was first stolen from her. She subsequently exhibited it in several museums before selling it at auction with Christies's in NY. The painting is now safely residing again in a private collection.

Another work stolen from the author's gallery in San Francisco in 1984, titled *Study for the River at Ascutney*, was recovered thanks to an astute collector who happened to encounter it for sale approximately 20 years later in a gallery, and remembered reading about its theft and looking at the image in one of the author's books: <u>Maxfield Parrish: The Masterworks</u>. The collector notified the author, who in turn called the police and asked them to pick up the painting in the gallery that was exhibiting it.

Based on the author's knowledge, there is a Parrish oil titled *Girl Skiing*, dated 1931, which had been used as a cover for <u>Ladies Home Journal Magazine</u>, which disappeared from a New York gallery under unexplained circumstances. When the owner of record went to retrieve it, the gallery surmised that it had been stolen since it wasn't available to be returned. It remains missing.

The most egregious of the Parrish works thefts occurred in Los Angeles when two murals that Parrish had created as part of a commission for Gertrude Vanderbilt Whitney disappeared, stolen in July 28, 2002 in a daring theft reminiscent of the movie *The Thomas Crown Affair*. According to the FBI and the police that investigated the theft, the thieves cut a hole in the ceiling of the gallery, disarmed the alarm system, rappelled two stories down and cut the two five and a half feet by eight and a half feet canvas paintings out of their massive frames, rolled them up and exited the way they had come in through the hole in the ceiling of the building. These two works are listed in the FBI's "World's Ten Most Valuable Art Works Still Unrecovered". It was theorized at the time that someone had paid to have them stolen and that they are now hidden in someone's private mansion.

As of the time of this book's publication, a Parrish oil done in the first decade of the 20th century mysteriously disappeared from a vault where it had been stored for nearly 20 years. Its whereabouts has been determined and it is in the process of being recovered by its owner as of this writing.

Many of the pieces of art mentioned in this book were at one time or another housed in the Cornish Colony Museum which the author founded in 1998.

The back cover photo of the author was taken on the grounds of the Cornish Colony Museum.

The front cover photo of *Dingleton Farm* courtesy of the Parrish archives of Alma Gilbert.